THE MONDAY RHETORIC
OF THE LOVE CLUB

The Monday Rhetoric of the Love Club is an entertaining collection of short stories and dialogues by the American poet Marvin Cohen whose previous book *The Self-Devoted Friend* was very well received. Mr Cohen had a beguiling talent and in this collection proves once more that fantasy does not have to be divorced from the practical business of life. His tales – though surrealist in form – always take off from the most everyday affairs and are buoyed up by the author's humour and wonderful facility with words. It will be a long time before the reader forgets the title story, with its pathetically funny routine recreations of sexual adventures, or *Saving Art for Tourism* which tells of the lunatic devotion of a small town to the crumbling monument which is its one attraction; but perhaps most memorable of all is *Listening to Herman*, a wild extravaganza on the prosaic enough subject of a party bore. Marvin Cohen creates his own world but one soon recognises that the themes he plays over and sheds new light on through the originality of his version are loneliness, heartache, inadequacy and the whole range of human folly, with which we are all familiar.

By the same author

THE SELF-DEVOTED FRIEND

Marvin Cohen

THE MONDAY RHETORIC OF THE LOVE CLUB
and other parables

A NEW DIRECTIONS BOOK

Library of Congress Catalog Card Number: 72-93979

Some of the pieces in this collection were first published in
New Directions in Prose and Poetry, numbers 19 and 21 and
are included by permission of the Publisher.

First published clothbound (ISBN: 0-8112-0474-X) and as New
Directions Paperbook 353 (ISBN: 0-8112-0475-8) in 1973

Printed in Great Britain; bound in the United States of America

New Directions Books are published for James Laughlin
by New Directions Publishing Corporation,
333 Sixth Avenue, New York 10014

For my mother and father; also
for Audrey Nicholson who kindly
helped edit this book.

CONTENTS

Magazines and anthologies in which some of these parables, stories, fables, dialogues, pieces, and prose-poems have previously appeared: *Panache*, (English) *Vogue*, *Sumac*, *Ambit*, *Dialogues*, *Transatlantic Review*, *Twentieth Century*, and *New Directions* Annuals.

ON THE CLOCK'S BUSINESS AND THE CLOUD'S NATURE

What is a cloud?
A cloud is a clock on vacation.
Oh. It wanders irresponsible?
Yes, it relaxes.
When does it return?
When the clock has to start working again.
For whose benefit?
For the office clerks whose foreman is strict about time.
Oh. What happens to the cloud that the clock *was*?
Its vacation was dissolved, and so it was restored into a hard clock.
With any sign of regret?
Not visibly. It must be wound up and click like clockwork, so it had no time to mourn the passing of its cloud self.
It sounds pretty busy.
It *is*, and meets itself at the end of a circle.
Where is *that*?
Depends on what time it is; it's got to be accurate.
Why? Why the precision?
The commercial world would collapse without it. A *cloud* can go gather its wool, but a *clock* has got to be on time. And there's no second thought about it, or a moment's hesitation. It's up to a clock to prove itself, and be on the wall. (I mean 'ball,' but 'wall' too.) If the office workers are caught watching it, the foreman will punish them.

For that matter, if those office workers look out the window at the *cloud*, and gaze in reverie, doesn't the demon foreman give them punishment for *that*? Clock and cloud have a point in *common*, there!

Yes, but don't confuse the two. A clock is a clock.

Oh, so what's a cloud?

A clock on vacation.

Then a clock is a cloud whose vacation is over. Back to the old office routine. Is that right?

Yes. Business goes by clocks. Leave the *poets* to the *clouds*.

Are poets, by nature, idle?

Sure. Hence their addiction to clouds.

Oh. Then poets are rovers.

Purposelessly. But: who goes by a clock, has got to be on time. He's *appointed*.

Oh. What appointment does he have to keep?

It's urgent, whatever it is. The clock would guarantee that.

Oh. Whereas a cloud – is a lack of stress.

Slack, I'd call it. And lazy.

Oh. The cloud has license?

It lingers the day long. It loiters. It plays hooky, and gets away with it. Really, it's aimless.

What's business's aim?

To justify the clock.

For how long?

Indefinitely. Businesses are self-perpetuating. They operate on their own profit.

What does a *cloud* earn?

Nothing. It *is* earned.

How?

It's a vacation. You must *earn* a vacation.

How?

By working hard for it!

How?

By going round the clock.

Oh. Is a clock round?

Yes. And continuous.

When does it break off?

For a vacation.

Oh. It softens up?

Yes. It floats away. Cloudlike.

THE TRUTH PRESERVED IN VERBAL CUBICLES OF ICE, TO FREEZE OUT THE MELTING CHARGES OF THE CRIME OF GOSSIP

I

On a ship traveling in the North Sea, two of the passengers were women gossips, who talked along the whole route. Beginning from the bottom of Africa, and continuing high up the North Sea. Their babbling went on and on. They outbabbled the waves.

It got colder and colder, the more and more northern they sailed, but on they blabbered, taking no notice.

Meanwhile, they kept on drawing north. Nor did their talk decrease. It increased.

The route sailed colder and colder. But bare due north, the boat continued to travel.

The other passengers huddled in their cabins, to keep warm. The *crew* were wise enough to keep indoors, as well.

But not those two women gossips. Impervious to the chill, they were warmed up by the heat of their conversation, which flared *incessantly,* without letdown. No silent syllable was heard.

The North Pole grew near. Still, the boat climbed. With the women gossips exposed on the windswept deck, like weather-beaten fixtures, the whole route long.

They reached a frozen climate. Still, they yapped on. The waves tossed ice at them.

The atmosphere changed. A dangerous level had been reached. Exposure had been carried too far north.

Something happened to the two women's words. The words were all freezing, in mid-air, just as delivered. Long words, short words, words of every description and vowel, without exception – they all froze.

And then, subsequently, their *echoes* froze. The women, animated, prattled gaily on. They were suffused with the ardor and sweat of their discourse and interchange.

But words of ice can't be heard. So they began not to hear each other.

This imposed a silent pall on the conversation that otherwise had been so lively.

II

The boat docked on the North Pole, through ice floes. Penguins and seals, millions of years old, were fresh preserved by the extreme cold. Like food kept alive in a refrigerator.

The ship's business was done. Then all passengers reboarded, after their chilly touring excursion, for the trip due south.

The return voyage was merry. The frozen words and their echoes that the two gossips had uttered on deck now began to thaw. And when they melted audibility was sounded in an incessant rain of prattle to drench and deluge all ears. So the flood waxed, as the tide turned mirthfully.

III

The words melted so well, that not only were they fluent, but fluid. They were from hot Latin Mediterranean tongues.

All the passengers crowded the decks to overhear last week's words of ice now turned to melted sound. But what was said hardly could be said to melt the passengers – *or* the crew, for that matter! The gossip was exposed. It was like a playback from a concealed tape recorder, and those two gossips had shrilly, even maliciously, concocted scandal to spice the fiction of each passenger and crewman. How unpopular the gossips now were, their lies exposed to blatant indignation! They were harangued, crowded to the rails, spat at. The passengers, to a man, vowed revenge. Even the captain, whose character had been maligned and morality impugned, was not loathe to stick out a plank for the gossips to walk blindfolded on, to tumble drowningly at the end. It was an unruly mob of passengers, thirsty for revenge. An improvised court tried the gossips, and a guilty verdict had plentiful evidence, for some of the harder-frozen bits of gossip and iced echo cakes were only now turning to melt, revealing such busybody tongues of wicked reincarnation as to stun the righteousness of each Godloving victim. Half of the passengers understood the gossips' language and were only too glad to translate for the other half. The translation made the tone more devastating, and the content filthier.

The gossips were accused of being gossips. They were both a middle-aged lady. The husband of one had been killed in a war, the husband of the other was in jail. Their children already had just married, so they were free, these ladies, to injure the reputations of whoever they found about. And what better source material than an oceanliner?!

IV

The accused now pleaded their defense. Their only defense was: "It was nothing but truth that we said. So why punish us? Why waste ice to preserve a lie? Ice is *valuable,* it keeps food fresh. It was the *truth* we froze, and not anything we made up."

One by one, the passengers, shamefaced, had to drop the case, and withdraw their prosecution. Also were the crew members abashed, and ceased from pushing their legal action (roughly unofficial as it was, so crudely improvised), as a tacit confession, amounting tantamount to an admission, that alas the gossips were correct, but let nothing more be said about the matter, and may vapor wisp the words away. The crestfallen passengers were proved guilty.

How did it all come about? The gossips had big ears. They heard. With their big eyes, they saw. With their brains, they cynically compounded. And how did the elements cooperate, in working out, in stages of state, what these ladies took pains to discover, and convert to the merciless veracity of tongue?

From air to ice to water, was the process and revelation of their grave words damning and defeating those passengers condemned to what they did by the observant factfinding gossips. Anything committed had found its way into the gossips' net. Unearthed. Air first the gossips spoke. And ice it turned to. And fire made water out of it, like tears of guilty confession, when temperate suns melted those tales told of temptations so undergone that the damage was done, and the chronicle made available by the voluble pair of historians. Having melted, may those words evaporate. Once released, that record can't be repeated. And the southbound ship, with the gossips vindicated, grew into hot climate. But not so hot as what had been divulged, on the passage north.

THE SAVING OF SURREALISM

Who was feeding Surrealism while all the poets were taking the afternoon off to watch the conclusive championship ball game on millions of identical television sets? I was one of them, I was watching too, when in alarm, and a deadening pang, I realized that Surrealism was being left unattended, and was missing the many warm meals it required just to stay alive on one Sunday afternoon! I panicked. Should Surrealism die of this mass criminal neglect, all the poets would have to fall back to imitating Alfred Lord Tennyson, which would be a blow against the future and an unexpected square meal fed to all the ghosts of reaction. (And that would be all those ghosts would need to come alive and haunt us in their bodies again!) So there was no time to lose, an emergency was at hand that gave even me a sense of responsibility. I left the television set still giving out the latest images of the game in progress (which was so exciting that it tempted me to remain, so I had to tear myself loose like Odysseus resisting the Sirens), and ran down the apartment building till I alighted on the street. Then without stopping I ran to the Surrealism Center, which is a big building with a cell in the middle, where the Surrealism unicorn is kept in strict and well-fed custody by its devoted guardians. Much to my horror, all the guardians had gone off to watch the game as well; and it gave me a cosmic stomach ache to see the Surrealism beast lying on its side, belly swollen, with an emaciated look in its eyes, and the boils of starvation growing regularly between the hairs of its skin. I had to rescue it, or the entire Avant-Garde would go down the drain! There was no time to lose, as the death rattles were growing closer. No food was handy, so I would have to feed it myself — first I put an arm in its mouth, and slowly it sucked it off. That was an appetizer, or an hors-d'oeuvre. Then went in my whole leg on the same side of me as that eaten arm. The monster of Surrealism made quick work of that dainty leg, taking a nice hunk of nourishment by gently amputating it right up to the corresponding ball on that lateral side of the body. It was making a quick recovery; and modern poets would have my martyrdom to thank when critics would attribute their styles to the surrealist influence. I was saving the world for Surrealism — or was it vice versa? But History was angry at me, for History would have liked to close the case on Surrealism to have it done with to make a serene verdict on that period or art movement from an interpretive and analytical position in the rectitude of retrospect. Momentarily, I had deprived History of this advantage, but didn't fear retribution from *that* quarter, as I had Surrealism already at work devouring me in the present, which was mentally distracting to say the least. My other leg was now eaten up, for Surrealism's greedy and vigorous appetite was enjoying a speedy recovery. At this rate, I would soon be no more. I then began to spend more concern on Survival, for my own sake. It was selfish. I wanted to live, so as to be able to find out the result and details of the all-important ball game that was being decisively enacted on the television sets of poet and non-poet alike. I wanted the Yankees to win. I was already fed up with Surrealism. If only Surrealism could have been fed up with me! But no, it kept chewing away. All the pieces of me were absorbed in its digestive system. My problem was to put myself together. To my great and very good fortune, I found in the central pit of its belly a working television set. I turned it on, eagerly, and enjoyed, down to the last play, the entire second half of the ball game whose progress I had been forced to abandon when realizing that my current devourer (whose lodger I was) would be dead of starvation unless I acted. Well, I *had* acted. My promptness had saved all of poetry from an unmitigated disaster, as well as art of course. But it had cost me the wholeness of my body. (Nothing good or heroic is without its awful price.) Yet it hadn't deprived me of watching the crucial climax of the ball game, thanks to the interior preparedness and sporting domesticity of my homekeeping monster of Surrealism. I had my cake, and was eaten too. The story ends happily, I'm glad to say. The Yankees won the championship, and that drove me mad with delight. It was a disembodied glee, a pure spirit of floating Yankee ecstasy as their posthumous rooter and well-rewarded fan, that dirged me melodiously – or all that remained of me – to a fulfilled grave on the Yankee side of Surrealism's ample plot. That's from where my voice is issuing, there being nothing else left of me but a saintly fame as the Saviour of Surrealism, and renown as a Yankee fan to the very death. Peace to all those above. I rest content.

LISTENING TO HERMAN

After dinner, we all sat around. We were gasping for our thoughts. A silence circulated, with comfort, and not anxiety, as the sponsor. Our bellies bulged in storage of recent acquisitions neatly stacked. Wine had induced optical swirling: the square ceiling revolved in slow circles. Drowsy waves of alert vitality subdued the circuit of tension. The blurred clarity of sweet images drooped on us. We chewed on candy, or sipped drops of burning brandy from glasses of transparent tulip.Our feet were not under us, but far forward.

Who spoiled our fine feast of contentment? Herman, the loquacious bore. "That reminded me," he said, apropos of nothing outside his head. "I was traveling, and had arrived at the station, when —" The rest were just banal words. Severing themselves from meaning, they floated in vocal clusters, sounds hazy in vapors of dull abstraction. Curse them: they all but murdered my serenity!

Indolence is so nice! The tranquility of lethargic musing. Bloated with eating, we dozed, or chased the soft butterfly from a dream suspended above. The fabric of woven imagery, so lovingly stitched together, was punctured by the uttered mutterings of vulgar tedium that Herman distributed with infinite largess. "The shoes this year are much more in fashion, don't you think, than those brogans or clods we tripped in last year? Slim shoes think, then . . . impart grace to the dancer — a partner congratulated me, and she said how soft I tread. But I *do* love spectator sports, don't you? Freud thinks that games are a substitute for war. I'm not as fit as I once was, but in my day I was considered a splendid athlete. I held a collegiate record that was only recently broken. Ah, say what you will, the current generation will be served! The papers report of a scientist with a new theory of death – a version so pessimistic, that it ought to drive people to religion. Heaven knows I'm not a churchgoer, but materialism is far too superficial to satisfy my mental needs. A philosopher said the other day that the soul was only a shallow pool. Well, I hope he slips in and drowns himself. This evening, I thought the fish course was excellent! And that white wine was so delicate! My diet has to observe a few restrictions, but otherwise the doctor is lenient. I caught a cold last week, but drowned it in citrus juice. I stayed home from work, and wiled away some delicious hours with a novel that ought to be banned for being erotic – though I'm plenty liberal, I can assure you. My wife and I consider ourselves humanists – right, dear? – and we're always warning whoever we can against confusing mere machines with the sacred souls of men. But in my opinion, the technological age contributes a prodigious amount to progress – and I defy any cynic to belittle the importance of scientific advancement. I bought my little tot a junior science set, and it intrigues him by the hour. He's quite talented when it comes to art, as well. The little heathen painted a nude female – I was shocked. But thank God it was almost abstract.

"Ah, it's so comfortable just lounging here. Excuse me. I opened the window a wee bit. Our health will circulate better now.

"You know, I must confess that I have a passion for music. I heard a symphony on the radio, and I hummed bars of it today. They flowed forth, as if my head were some uncanny phonograph needle. I'm also an excellent amateur photographer. I drove my family to the park last Sunday, and I shot nature in the raw – the trees were so natural, that they didn't seem posed. Nothing beats realism. Painting is at a dead end. And the prices in the art galleries! Fabulous! There must be a conspiracy. There's a culture boom. Reminds me of those war profiteers. Human nature is growing more corrupt by the minute. It makes you think twice, before accepting evolution. Last month I took my kid to the zoo. At one of the cages, he and a monkey whipped up a rapport. It was fun, and I felt very paternal for the both of them."

Herman's droning continuum was a verbal study in perpetual motion. He skipped from one subject to another like a frog in a fickle multitude of ponds. The host should have shut him up — but he was too polite to be obvious, and Herman ran on like a transcontinental train whose engine plows its own tracks. We were awake, and perfect passive captives to this monologue den of torture. All the air in the room was just a vocal passageway for Herman's tiresome pluckings of words out of context. The cliché machine bounced in abandon, to cover all subjects known to man. We were surfeited sick. We would turn desperado, and gag that compulsory maniac of talk. The rambling was non-stop in its voluminous greed.

Guest by guest, we all got up to leave. Herman took the cue in kind. To his taciturn wife, he gestured the 'let's go' signal. (Why hadn't he *said* it to her? I never could figure it out.) Our fatigued host thanked Herman for leading conversation into delightful broad byways. Herman was profuse in accepting this.

My wife and I got home, and released the babysitter. I couldn't sleep. Herman was speaking, in that unmistakable tone. Like a car siren that kept screaming, through mechanical default. Visually auditory words kept pouring from Herman's mouth. The monotone of rigid variation. My balance fell apart. I was going mad.

For distraction, I woke up my wife. She was sleepy, but a good sport. We had a tumble, but it barely entered into pleasure's zone. Like the cackle of static on a ruined radio program, Herman's voice zoomed up a steady staccato of interference. His voice was a rumbling world, roaring in at either ear. I couldn't shut off this deafening obsession.

Ear plugs were pathetically futile. The core of my skull was submitting these sounds.

Wave on wave: like an endless torment of hornets, swept down from clouds to sting and plague. The lips of articulation: Herman audible.

Not a snatch of sleep. Morning was a fuzzy day. It was grounded on Herman's undertone. Not a let-up. Within this repetition, insanity's independent rhythm grafted on a hookup, while I swayed. Bound by Herman's vocal cord, I endured an apprenticeship to lunacy, with monolithic perseverance. Heartlessly, I was barred from all variety alien to the intimacy of Herman's voice. In the wild din of silence, I heard it.

My wife worried to a hysterical pitch. To rid myself of those reiterative echoes was the puzzle pounding on me with a panic's gong of vibration. My system was pumping glandular heaves to the tone of that organic poison. My wife arranged a psychiatric appointment. But the psychiatrist was interested in recitations of my *childhood*! "That's *before* the fact, and bears no consequence," I rebelled. He insisted that his professional method was the correct one. Herman drowned him out. I abruptly left, without paying.

Anxiety for me made my wife neglectful of our boy. The problem was blown up into a domestic crisis. This acceleration was nightmare material.

After my second sleepless night, my wife's hysteria was converted by necessity into inspiration. The husband desperately needed rescuing. My work had been falling off, for the office was one loud buzz of Herman the day long. The boss had been alerted, becoming distrustful of my fidgeting, with the commercial minimum of sympathy. I was about to lose my job. Acute desperation, alarming her instinct for family survival, enlightened my wife with emergency's bolt of inspiration. "Go and visit him!" she declared. "Listen to him talk, all night. The reality will saturate, clutter, kill your memory. The obsession that's haunted you can only be purged by the real thing. Only Herman's presence can create a catharsis." Authority had made her summons imperious. I must heed it, to terminate delirium's crucifix that doubled between ordeal and agony.

I phoned up Herman. "Let's get together," I suggested. He invited my wife and me to dinner for the following night. I couldn't wait, so I asked him to visit us now. "That's impossible," he declared," I have a one-day attack of tonsilitis." My third sleepless night equipped me with special energy. Dinner with Herman would be curative, or else, I hoped, kill me off in haste. My ears were leaking pus. Cancer globules were forming there, breeding psychic pathology in all those little work cells. They were adroitly spelling out my doom.

I was wound up, as never before. Like an ancient Chinese

scroll of bureaucratic length being unrolled for academy inspection, the Herman machine unfurled the relentless intricacies of its tune. A pitiless unfolding, in murderous intensity. A compulsive mercilessness, scurrying in the sharp breeze of frenzy. It was too glaring for the dull solace of dizziness. Billions of infernal word variations were spawned on the eggnest theme of the chronic headache outbreak. The ruthless Hermanization of my head was proceeding on a national front, with strains of international grandeur intermingled. It was no simple jingle or pure melody. It was hell, boiled into sound, dripping slender serpents of malice, stirring the vipers' drops of a deadly vengeance.

We were at Herman's doorstep well before the appointment time. In ringing anticipation, his voice was making a production of my ears. My head was the gong, where he clanged all day. Like a metallic battering ram, the bruise rubbed precision on my nerve. Like a street drill or the dentist's instrument, it went like a wicked streak through my body.

"Come in," he welcomed, "right in here, where my wife is preparing drinks. My bout of tonsilitis has subsided. Heaven knows why I had it in the first place. The weather has been running eccentric these days, hasn't it? I can remember the weather of every day of my life – it's an uncanny trick of memory. But I wouldn't want to bore you with the recitation. Years of weather reports and outcomes are on active file – my head is a veritable weather bureau, but confines its forecasts to the predictable accuracy of the past. That reminds me that tomorrow is expected to be cloudy. No wonder my lumbago wart is stirring. I can stare at the clouds all day. It's fascinating, the number of patterns in all that shifting panorama. But at heart, I'm a sun-worshipper. I can lap it up. I go to the shore for it. I never vacation in the mountains. I love to go for a swim, and then let the sunbeams swim on me. Do you admire my tan? I'm glad, because I do. I always like my friends to share in my opinions. This confers a greater air of intimacy. And as we all know, harmony is the antidote against war. Do you know that the President was taken ill the other day? But the papers hushed it up. An acquaintance in the diplomatic corps discreetly informed me. The state of the economy is breathing too fast: I go in for a *gradual* fluctuation. When it comes to politics, I'm moderate right down the center. With this safe approach, I'm immensely farsighted. Foreign aggression is so potentially dangerous, I think the matter should be discussed in Congress. The United Nations has only feeble option to resist the inevitable dilemma that the world is facing. I just heard a television commentary warning against complacency. The speaker had a fascinating style of delivery. His hair I think was too much combed on one side. But my wife decided that he really had a handsome face. When it comes to men, I think women are better able to judge our appearance than our own mirrors. Do you like this suit? It was a bargain. Mostly, I'm ignorant of clothes; but I sure like what I wear. The other day I was walking down the street, and got stared at — by an impressive-looking woman! I was so flattered, my masculine pride went up. As a rule, it doesn't take much to keep my vanity alive. But I hate people who are sometimes slack in paying attention. Courtesy and consideration are only my due. I'm only human in asking for this right. I was told I talk too much, but only by an envious admirer whose mouth was too small to withstand the fatigue of enduring his own voice. My little son feeds a bird out the back window, but lately the bird hasn't reported for its meal. Perhaps it's a migratory tramp or something. My son's appetite has suffered. But at least mine is plainly all right. My wife eats whatever I do. That makes it so convenient.

"There, take that chair please. Begin eating, at once. I insist on no ceremony! We must be forward about these things.

"My dear, you're improving as a cook! Hearty congratulations are in order. I think food is basic to life, don't you? What can a starving man do? He's practically helpless!

"The more I think about it, the more my life is a fascinating achievement! When I was born, I was so inconsiderable! My mother, were she alive today, could talk for hours about my unrobust state of childhood. I spent my infancy with the tears rolling down my cute red cheeks. That was hardly fun, for the sensitive condition I was in. But *now* look at me! Who gets more out of life? I ought to be copied as a standard model. Fools would become wise, if they chose aspects of my life to studiously emulate. Not that I'm any sort of genius! No, I'm just *too* normal! A terrific combination of ingredients makes me dynamically balanced — I could go on and on. It's a subject I never tire of, so inexhaustibly manifest with possibilities that compel contemplation. But what about my dear guests? Are they having fun? What an insult to my elaborate hospitality, if this isn't the case."

My host was continuing. My head pounded its sockets loose. My wife looked at me with alarming concern. I stood up, and outshouted Herman, gaining the floor. It was the time the coffee was served. I went on, and kept going.

Herman was furious, but I didn't stop talking. What I spoke about was immaterial. I drew out its interminable length. The fury increased my pace.

My rate skyrocketed a verbiose marathon. My words packed space densely, like a huge monopoly machine. Herman's gorge choked to the brim with moral indignation.

While I kept sputtering out, Herman was on the phone to the police. He took an hour and a half explaining what he was complaining of, stopping occasionally to digress and branch out with chance expansion. Meanwhile, I was rivalling him in our joint counterpoint that shared a hideous assassination-rape of the mangled body of silence. Who knows whether the police sergeant had already hung up? Herman was pouring it on. His wife submissively smiled throughout. *My* wife tried a trivial interference. She was out competed, in a rugged contest of men locked in the no-rules mortality of a tongue-war.

Dawn was closing in. Neither Herman nor I could stop.

Wouldn't his throat choke of apoplexy? Wouldn't his throttle explode suddenly? Not his. He was brutally endowed.

Our sprawling wives slumbered in their chairs. Herman's kid was asleep in another room. At *my* home, the babysitter hadn't been relieved! My fourth night of no sleep had passed. I flamed into an embattled mass of fire.

I traded Shut up's, with my adversary. His practice and experience were beginning to tell. He slipped in several words for my one. My defense was slacking. The note of triumph entered Herman's voice.

I called on all my verbal reserves, and fought back with the weight of a rapidly decimating dictionary. Herman chose his words from a richer fund of resources. They lighted on me, like a pack of indiscriminate birds. His tongue was like a weather vane, tossing in a month of wild wind.

The spittle and the spleen also rose. The exchange closed quarters.

Then Silence crashed, like a lead ball, smashing the splintry floor. Our mouths kept moving, but all in a dumb-show. Phantom words were not given their heard bodily weight, but were mimed in the inarticulate panic of lips. Herman was like an epileptic. His oral pantomime screwed itself gulping. He strained to uncork the sound barrier.

Silence was vanquished. The words streamed at me, non-stop. (My own had ceased, like trickles from a dried-up river.)

Excruciating vowels were ejaculated, and jibbering consonants. I was being slaughtered, sent rocketing into annihilation!

Not a pause to break rhythm or rest its swell. Herman's being heard. Herman, I'm hearing you! Your wavelength is the sole one operating. You come through, sound is only you. The drum is rolling. My body is a splinter network of slightly-hinged bones. Each bone is your sound's familiar. Especially my top bone, with its revolving sockets. Oh Herman, I can see your sounds! Each one is a special burial bone!

THE BALANCE OF POWER

(Violence Without Meditation)

I met an important man. He looked down on me (a difficult accomplishment, considering my height) and when he spoke these words, they were underscored by command: "Go away." As we were in the free public street, owned jointly by policemen and politicians, I conveyed a note of courage in the answer, "No."

He hit me. With dignity and money, he hit me. While the hurt raised embarrassment from my blush, he snapped back his arm, preparing to repeat. My anger crushed him down, and when the blows stopped falling, he turned his surprise on me, and began retreating. I chased him, just for fun, since triumph delayed my step.

How proud I felt. How easy to survive. While returning home, I met an unimportant man. With insolence, I told him to go away. "Not right now," he answered.

A policeman took me to the hospital. It wasn't funny, but they had me in stitches. When released, I felt totally neutral.

The next man I saw, I said to him, "Don't be funny." "But I'm a comedian," he answered: "my livelihood." "So you're a professional," I retorted, and let his blood bounce softly off the pavement.

Next, I encountered a boxer. "Boy, you're strong," I said. "I must be," he replied, while a quick reflex made me dodge. Too late, and at once I found my skull. "You're hard," I cracked. "I must be," it answered; "and you're thick yourself."

With my skin loosely patched, I pounced along the street, alert to the trouble soon to assault me.

I made a fist, and kept it clenched. This squeezed the blood away, and soon the white knuckles grew blisters. Thus handicapped, I fell easy prey to my next would-be victim. My arms and legs lay sprawled beside me. After an imperfect matching job, I staggered upright, with a proud scorn twinkling in my virile eye. "How survived I am!" I managed to utter, just as my collapse caught up with me.

The hospital was white, like snow. I shook off the hovering angel, and sprouted new muscles. I walked out a new man.

"You're new," said the important man. "How changed," said the unimportant man. "Incredible," said the comedian. "What a comeback," exclaimed the boxer. "How annoying," crowed my would-be victim.

They made a path for me, while I chopped down a tree and poured the chips over my shoulder. "Knock it off!" I yelled. They fought among themselves, to be the first one.

Realizing that my legs were new, I tested them by running. They refused to stop, until safety was clutching at me with her ferocious arms.

Now, when I make love to safety, she calls me her favorite coward. I tell her what a wonderful nurse she is and she blushes.

A MOVEMENT, IN SEVERAL SHORT PAUSES (CONCLUDED BY ONE INTERMINABLE ONE)

Let's go somewhere.
I don't blame you.
Are you ready?
Not if you are.
Then we're all set.
That's for you to insist.
    (Pause)
What shall we do on the way?
Shop for an article.
A newspaper article?
No, a purchasing commodity.
You're too deep for me.
Yes, but I *feel* shallow enough.
    (Pause)
We've been walking.
I can tell.
Why? The distances we've covered?
Fatigue: Don't forget to mention *that*.
No. It's cost me my energy.
    (Pause)
I'm going to buy a left-handed handkerchief.
But what if your *right* nostril is on fire?
Tough. It fends for itself then.
Are you *always* this unfair?
That's not a fair question, I warn you.
Then I'll disregard the answer you're not going to give.
    (Pause)
Have we arrived?
I don't know. What's our destination?

It depends on where we're going.
Depends! Can't you be sure about *anything*?
Not when *uncertainty* casts its ugly doubt.
(*Pause*)
Let's stop. We've walked enough.
Why? What tells you that?
The perspiration is using my clothes as a sieve.
What *more* evidence do you have?
The bottom of my feet are where my soles used to be.
Then put on your shoes, next time.
(*Pause*)
Are we there now?
'There' can be anywhere. So 'here' is no better than the
next place.
But not worst neither, no, sure?
Don't get plain with *me*.
I'm only helping out.
Yes. That's why you're a hindrance.
(*Pause*)
It's my limit. Not a step more.
Are you *stubborn*, or merely *obstinate*?
Whichever way resists any further advance.
Then you force *me* to stop, as well.
Why? Are you a *shadow* of some sort?
Granted. But more substantial than its object, if you're the
object I cast.
Don't confuse me. I don't know light from dark.
No need to, if you can tell time.
But my clock always stops.
That means you don't *feed* it enough.
Why should I? It's only a *small* one.
(*Pause*)
Are we at the end?
Yes. The road stops where I stop.
Is your approach to geography *always* so personal?
When I'm tired, geography quits whirling and settles down.
But people *depend* on geography for their whereabouts.
When you stop, you stall billions of lives.

Blame the *earth*, if it puts *me* foremost.
You're not foremost: I'm *equal* with you. *(They're parallel*
    to each other; they stand without moving)
Not one more step forward.
How long will our stillness last?
Forever, provided I say one word.
What magic word is that?
This: *Curtain!*
    (Curtain)

RAIN'S INFLUENCE ON MAN'S ATTITUDE TO ART

A man and wife hated culture. But it suddenly rained hard, while they were passing a museum. So they only had a dry reason for entering.

Is that how the conflict was solved?

Yes. They shook some of the rain off on culture, while culture gave *them* a brief soaking.

Who gains, in the long run?

The rain. It lasts longer.

Than the couple?

And than the priceless treasures in the museum.

Oh. Where *was* the museum, by the way?

In the middle of an empty desert. *True* art is hard to come by.

But doesn't the attendance suffer, when public art is isolated in an ivory tower?

That protects art's scarcity. Once its rarity is ruined, devaluation would set in.

Would that depreciate the assets?

Yes. Products become cheap, when too much democracy is inserted.

Oh. Where did the culture-hating couple go, once the rain dried up?

They were offered jobs as mummies. Their future was guaranteed.

So it was fatal for them to enter the museum.

Yes, but it beats standing in the rain.

What harm could rain have done? Is water impure?

They would have become fishes. That would have stunted evolution, reversed its laborious growth, and necessitated its beginning all over again, from the sea on.

That's tough. Another museum down the drain.

Yeah. What time gives, time can take away.

Who loses, in the end?

People, and their predecessors.

Is it so sad it's hopeless?

More than that. It's miserable.

God. I'm raining down tears.

You need distraction. I'll take you to a museum.

What's there to see?

Nothing, unless you mop out the ocean that swims in little waves from those prehistoric craters in your eyes.

I wish something wonderful could devour me.

Only because you've failed to *be* the devourer of something wonderful.

Oh Why were they married, by the way?

The couple who were buried in the museum to avoid the rain?

Yeah.

To form a cultural unit, an institution so self-sufficient that outside culture wouldn't be necessary.

Yeah, but the culture they hated wasn't outside. It was *inside* the museum.

Sure. Art is too delicate not to need a roof.

Like man an umbrella.

Right. It's destructive to be too vulnerably exposed.

Then you condemn the elements?

Sure. Rain foremost.

CONFUSIONS FOR EMBROIDERING DETECTIVE INTRIGUES

There's an exclusive detective who only takes on cases that have *already* been solved. I admire his ingenuity.

Yes, but his soft job is a lazy sinecure. Does it require any skill?

No, only audacity.

And it's devoid of *thrills*, isn't it?

Yes. There's not much suspense in it.

(*Pause*)

I know a detective who's so exclusive, he only handles cases that don't even have a *problem* to be solved.

Then why are they called 'cases'?

Short for 'briefcases'. You see, he carries a portfolio without being an ambassador.

Oh. That explains it.

(*Pause*)

I know a detective who's investigating himself.

On what grounds?

His own. He does it in his own back yard.

Why? Can't he afford an office?

Yes, but he insists on operating a *charitable,* rather than profit-able, business.

But—

And 'charity,' he declares, 'begins at home.'

Oh. Has he found any evidence?

Yes. The investigation has been successful. He's been placed under house arrest.

What evidence incriminated him?

The hunch that he had done something wrong.

But what did he do that was wrong?

Nothing. But he needed practice.

(Pause)

Won't his career suffer?

No; it was a brilliant piece of detective work.

Was it written up in the newspapers?

No, they had already gone to press when the publicity was released.

Oh. Then with no fame, who will hire him?

He *invents* clients.

Invents! Does he have a license?

That's invented, as well.

Doesn't he take too much on himself?

That's his style. And a man's style is his signature. You can't argue with it.

You mean he has a *signature*, as well?

Yes, but only when his name is working.

(Pause)

THE WORLD IS ALL CLUTTERED WITH OBJECTS

The world is all cluttered with objects.
Where? Isn't this stage bare?
Well, *we*'re here, aren't we?
We? Who are we?
We're the ones who, if it weren't for us, the stage would be empty.
That's not a flattering function, as a reason for my whole existence. Just to take up space isn't why I'm proud to have been once created.
But you're solid. The air stops flowing, when it bounces off your surface. It can't pass through you. You're so opaque, the audience can make you out. *(Looks at audience with look of sympathy)* You're as physical an object as a stage prop. And even more personally real, when you consider your animation. Your properties are those that belong to the living. But enough of you. I had meant to mention things more general than yourself alone.
I'll do you the same disservice, some day.
My subject had started out to be the world at large, with the various things in it.
Sweeping generalizations will get you nowhere.
But still, the world is a striking fact, if you get around to it.
The *world*? Oh, it's *there*. *(Shrugs complacently)* But why bother to acknowledge it?
So as not to be ungrateful. We wouldn't have a leg to stand on, if the world didn't help to support it.
Well, your theories sure aren't groundless, anyway.
The world is the undeniable basis of all reality.
Yes, it sure does interfere with my dreams.
Dreams? Why waste time dreaming, when the world offers

more truth than we can ever learn in a total lifetime of years?

Truth is dull, when it gets plentiful. It's really a diluting agent, like water in a whiskey glass. Dreams keep us drunk. You, you can drink water. But being sober isn't so much fun. The world appears better, when converted to imagination: it's more translated in terms of *us*. Me, I'm the measure of the world, by passing it through my dreams. Otherwise, truth is merely a dull irritant.

But are you insulting reality?

Reality is too well established to stop operating on the strength of a passing insult. Leave me to my unreal mind. If the world amuses you, you can keep *my* portion, too. Just stop referring to it. Thank God, our stage is empty. It's more than I can merely bear, to suffer us alone.

There's more than just us. What of the clothing we're wearing? They're our closest approximate environments. They're our outward trappings, our physical surroundings. Look, watch me move: *(Waving arms, walks a few paces)* Where I go, they go, too.

That limits your constitutional freedom. But dreams exist in a rare purity, devoid of a cluttered environment. It affords peace, for concentration.

In a vacuum?

No. The material is plentiful, I assure you.

Well, it's the world for me.

Take it. I'll go the other way. *(They part, each going off to opposite end of stage. Bareness remains, then curtain)*

A SHADOW SPEECH PLAY

If a shadow is developed in a darkroom, it can cast an *object*.

Does it cast the same object that *it* was cast by when out in the sun?

Oh, stop being technical. It *forgot* what it came from. It only wishes to create.

An artist? But an artist paints a *picture*, not an object.

No. This is a *shadow*, that creates a specific object.

Isn't that overdoing the *modern* bit?

So what? Progress has *got* to be made.

(*Pause*)

Why are you so interested in shadows? Your fascination is almost morbid.

Because they're cooler and darker than the freckle-faced world. They're underdogs, as well. Everybody's treading them underfoot.

Why can't shadows fend for themselves, instead of being help-less?

Because they practice humiliation.

Why don't they rise and revolt? They suffer the sun's yoke.

To overthrow what they're dependent on would be to slice off their own necks. A parasite's survival depends on keeping the thing it leeches off so healthy, that there's surplus to afford.

But don't shadows play primarily a secondary role?

Only compared to the sun-lit objects that are predominant. Subordination doesn't *keep* the shadow down: it develops the shadow's profile, and fills it out with sweet fat.

Then shadows, like beggars, must thrive?

Sure. But their masters must do so first.

(*Pause*)

My vision is elevated. It's the *sun* I'm thinking of.

As long as you remain modestly *thinking* of it; don't fall into the error of assuming that you *are* it.

No. I know my place. No good to get elevated ideas.

Quite right. You don't want to burn yourself out when you're so young.

Yes, that would be a mistake.

Be cool, and play it safe.

I'll accept my lot's being humble. Let those who wish to stumble seek more exalted footing.

Yes. But don't become complacent for being so *low*.

No. That's only adding *perversion* to arrogance.

You're getting sensible.

That's what comes with agreeing with you.

Then are you ready for my quiz?

As ready as summer is, to locate the sun so democratically central that most nations on almost all the continents can be kissed by radiance of so well-distributed a bestowal.

You gild your rhetorical lily. Come down, and sniff a little moonblaze. You have a gold-stroke, that only silver can remedy. The sun is cracked with some of your craze.

Then quench my glaze with a little question's glitter; unless it fazes me, I'll catch it with a quiver.

You see those long inclining shadows? (*Points*) Filling the alley's dusty emptiness? Isn't that somehow a *Sunday* scene? But fact dictates this day as Wednesday. Why are *Sunday* shadows different from Wednesday ones? – assuming equality in season and hour of afternoon.

Because they've had four days to complete their decaying.

You reply too cynically. Here, try this: De*fine* a shadow. I mean its inmost, non-surface, self.

A shadow? Why, that's a soiled replica of the original object. It was cast, but not as solidly.

But why is an object more solid than its shadow?

Because it's flattered with more direct personal attention by people. This inflates its pride, and makes it a substantial citizen.

Somehow, you're not being scientific.

No need to be. Objects and shadows speak for themselves,

separately. I eye them with spectator disdain. But were *I them,* I'd feel haunted with paranoia.

That's too human an attribute for them to assume. But if you were the *sun,* what would you say?

I'd say not once, but continually, "Why can't I ever find an object to be an intermediary between myself and my shadow?" Frantically, I'd question the air. But not one human sprite would venture even a *puny* reply.

But what language would you, as a sun, be speaking?

(*Imperiously*) Total language.

Very impressive. But is your 'total language' visual?

It lies bleeding in the sky, scourged by innumerable semantic battles.

Then will you retreat, and undergo a sunset?

Certainly. It's my grand coup. For, once I've set, all four horizons, that eye can see at one fill, are plunged purely into the total darkness of shadow. My deputy, the moon, has but a wan rage. Mighty night is my blackest creation. Against it, man defies with thousands of neon bulbs. What candle is that trivial defiance of my intense power! (*Walks haughtily off*) Good night.

(*Darkness*)

BECOMING A BUILDING AFTER CONSIDERING AN APPROACH TO A PREVIOUS BUILDING

I

Have you been to that big wonderful building yet?
(*Looks at it*)
    No. I'm waiting for *it* to come to *me*.
    You might have to wait a long time.
    (*Looks at watch*) Well, I've got fifteen minutes, anyway.
    But the building is a couple a centuries old.
    So?
    Well, that tends to cripple its moving. It can't get around now so much, you know.
    What a senile old stick-in-the-mud!
    Still, even *modern* buildings don't move around much.
    Laziness! The present generation is the idlest—.
    But some *prefabricated* houses are mobile.
    Well, good for them. They're enterprising.
    Do you see *every*thing in business terms?
    No. I consider leisure completely separate.

II

    Come, aren't we going to that splendid building?
    What! Are you *still* reminding me?
    But you don't know what's *inside* it.
    I only know things from the *outside* first. I approach things gradually.
    That's mighty cautious of you.
    Yes. Even people. First I see them from the outside. I know

their superficial appearance before I know them inside.

Good. Then you're no intruder.

No. I wouldn't presume.

Is there *anything*, or *anyone*, you first knew from the inside before knowing from the outside?

Yeah. My mother.

Which did you prefer?

In, frankly.

But wasn't there a relative lack of objectivity?

That was hardly my concern, at that time.

When did you *begin* burdening your shoulders with responsibility?

As soon as there was *room* on the shoulders.

Why? What had to be removed?

Chips, you see.

Oh. Now shall we approach that building? (*Looks at it*)

No. Let's wait for it to come this way.

But we might have to wait *forever*!

No. I'm a busy man. I can't be bothered.

Then we'll visit the building?

Yes. On our own steam.

Well? Why don't you begin walking?

(*Legs are gone. Concrete rectangular tube up to the torso, instead*) I can't. I've just become a building myself—more recent than that one.

Then you must be given a postal *address*.

Sure. My name would make the beginnings of one.

Where? I don't see any sign.

(*Other man has become a building, about eight feet tall, with a flat front and large windows. It doesn't move. The lights are on; then they blank out*)

IMAGE STREAMLINING

I was once a public relations man. My first client was a cockroach. I was so surprised to see him.

Him?

Well, *it*, I suppose: it's hard to tell.

Go on with your story.

As I said, I was in public relations. I had just opened shop. A cockroach – dressed quite well if you please – walked in nonchalantly.

Why nonchalantly?

It was his cool approach.

Oh. *(Pause)* Continue, please.

The cockroach spoke quite distinctly. I was grateful: usually I have difficulty with foreigners.

But a public relations man is supposed to *adjust*.

Well, so I entered business under a slight handicap.

Enough of *you*: tell about the cockroach.

"Can you improve our image?" he asked. "Whom do you represent?" I replied, with professional detachment.

So what did the cockroach say to *that*?

He said, "I represent the United Cockroaches of America. We're a thoroughly unionized organization. We're even a chartered corporation, to please the capitalists."

Clever, those cockroaches. So what did *you* answer?

I said, "To the point: What do you want?"

Go ahead.

So the little insect replies, "Sir, we seem to disgust people. They don't see how harmless we are. They're squeamish, they look down on us. Those stuffy morons! We want to be more seemly. We want to erect our dignity on a noble carriage."

Did the cockroach go to *school?* — that's quite a mouthful.

He was educated, all right. But I didn't feel inferior: after all, I towered *over* him.

(Looking at other) You're a brave man, all right. *(Pause)* Were you of any help to him?

I quoted my fee. I said it would involve extensive research. But that I would give him most considered and careful advice. He persisted, that he *did* require my services. So he signed a contract to that effect.

I'm glad to see that you don't discriminate against clients.

Of course not. Prejudice is fatal, businesswise.

But didn't the *nature* of your client sort of give you the creeps?

I repressed it; I acted like a routine course was pursued.

Your professional ethics are excellent. Did you carry on the market research campaign? Was it exhaustive? What were your findings?

I did all that. I spared no method, down to the finest detail.

Then did you call the little squirt in?

I did: he was breathless with panic. I had to lend him a damp sponge: he was soaking with liquid excretion.

Ugh! A little accident of nature.

I did him the courtesy of pretending ever so faintly not to notice.

Weren't you too conspicuous about it?

Don't be ridiculous. "Your result!" he clamored. Cautiously, I began: "Publicity is not an exact science. In *your* case, it's the *lack* of publicity that is here heartily recommended." "But doctor — my species can hardly make themselves scarce — there's too many of us. Doctor — it's our *image* we want to improve." "Pay me the fee," I said, "and receive the findings." It was an exorbitant amount. With meticulously enunciated agony, choked with a note of despair, the little creep again asked, "Doctor! Advise us!"

This suspense is awful! What *was* your advice?

"In the interests of your public image," I said — and here's the crux of the matter — "Off with your legs?"

(Aghast) And how did he take it?

Bit me . . . Here. (*Showing cheek*)
Well — those are your occupational hazards.
(*Proudly*) It's worth it! I'm entirely devoted to my job!

SAVING ART FOR TOURISM IN
ONE TRAGIC LESSON

Deep in one of this world's wealthiest, most ancient and traditional continents (famous for its variety of national tongues, especially those of the western Romance languages) stands a town not quite large enough to be called a city. This town, set by an idle, mud-pent river between a sloping range of valleys, would have been obscure and undistinguished; and it is, except for a unique item in it, prized beyond the rest of its drearily unextraordinary self.

Somewhere approximately to the middle of the town's center stands — or pretends to stand — a venerable religious relic mentioned reverently in all tourist guide books as a universal attraction for visitors. All other buildings contemporary with this shrine have long since been dissolved in time's dust. But *this* antique has weathered all the ages. Successive coats of paint have faded into one another, the wood has peeled, the metal has splintered, the stone is pore-riddled like sponge, the ornamental surfaces are rubbed away; but there it is, having tolerably survived, to its increasing fame and glory, a requisite 'must' for foreign culture-addicts.

Otherwise, the town itself is dull. The other buildings are all shabbily recent, of an uninspiring motley of architectural drabness. The movie theatres play antiquated Westerns born at the inception of cinematic mediocrity. Go along the streets: the ice cream parlors cheat you, for cheap bread-crumbs are intermingled in so-called ice cream. The coffee is so stale that the locals call it tea. The beer tastes like semi-urinated lemon water. The wine must have been blood crushed from ants by the coarse, unshod feet of drooping-jawed rustics. As for the 'meat', steers would die laughing, and steer clear of the dubious incest of 'eating' this unrefrigerated breed of extinct leather.

Internally, the town was not a money-maker; its own citizens were not good domestic providers. The only dependable revenue was its tourist trade, all due to that particular monument for which every conscientious traveler routes his global itinerary. But since conscientious travelers are too few, or are not wealthy enough to make the out-of-the-way scenes and so must confine their holiday excursions to the great old large cities where so much is concentrated in one whirling visit, the scale of tourism for this town was modest, its natives subsisting on the margin of poverty's eking standard.

The Chamber of Commerce makes a small, neat profit. The restaurant, café, hotel, postcard, and souvenir trade keep the coffer tills just full enough with shekels from international sight-seers. The religious building is their golden calf. It's invaluably old: its decay works for them. (In the town, old people are given the right of way in the streets, hats tipped off to them.)

But things that decay are likely to fall, soon or late. This is one of nature's laws that are artificially defended against, in the pre-vention-over-cure creed of conservation. Municipal watchdogs keep a weather eye on the precarious monument. A crack electri-cian is hired on a round-the-clock basis to divert any bolt of lightning from that delicate edifice. The town has commissioned an anti-war lobby in the national legislature, since a bombing raid would doom the precious attraction, level it from sight and destroy its utility as an unbeatable fund-raiser. Geology experts scratch the soil with anti-earthquake rods that thwart excitable rock. Barricades to keep out natural hazards have been pre-cisely instrumented. No bacteriological colony of virus, capable of contaminating obsolete matter by malignant agency, may be bred to infest these carefully sterilized premises. Tourists must take a health test (sneezing and coughing illegal on forfeit of fine) before being permitted so far as the highly sanctified inner gate, where a binocular view hints at the riches in store. Germ carriers are weeded out in a ruthless warfare of chemical censorship. Suppression of alien infiltration spares only the bona fide tourist, on a generous quota system of widely popular exclusiveness. Nothing remotely harmful may venture close to that sole source of fitful income for the total inhabitants of a town. The very weather is daily checked by umbrella-clad philosophers whose theories conservatively practise a dry goal. Rainfall is forbidden to molest the natural self-weathering of this time-hallowed shrine, this mecca of the tourist sport.

One day, an alarmed guard reports to the Mayor's vigilant committee of minute-aldermen that the foundations are gradually giving way. The building seems in a slump. Its base-support slopes; the land seems to slide free. Stones are slipping loose: pebbles shoot out from underneath. Moss slime and the pus of moodx vegetation betray a decomposing factor: putrefaction confounds esthetically scented nostrils. "It's a rotten matter," tersely concludes the report. The heavens frown ominously. Test winds are unleashed. The building totters with every sharp breeze, swaying like an aspen, quivering like a tubercular epileptic.

Venerable decay, or the evidence thereof, is excellent for tourism; but the very existence itself of the relic must surely be preserved from perishing! Or else the town's economics would dip below zero freezing!

Clang went the emergency gong; to their collective feet rose a community. On the unseen enemy, it was all-out war!

This celebrated temple of an outmoded religious function from a holy era, seems not long for this world! Quickly, a panic conference is called by the local chieftains. If tourism's source is cut off, the town itself is due for the poorhouse, a charity case beyond redemption.

This building, however infirm, must hold the fort, whatever the windy odds! Economic survival is at stake. The town's inconsequential name would be wiped off the revised editions of every self-respecting map atlas! (Rarity ceases to be dear, when the rare object loses its existence; the word's ungrateful memory demotes it to a myth.) To cope with this desperation, the town's most powerful heads linked brains in a crusade, a campaign of great renown: 'To conserve' was the verb these burghers agreed on. Now only technical execution became the abiding problem.

Outside the town, a different type of excitement was working. A flurry of fermented agitation was converging broadly on that archaic magnet that worried the town fathers so! An ingress of money was on the way!

Rumor spread with rampant acceleration. Its hot news penetrated all travel agencies within the commercial spread of civilization. Contagion spawned foamy waves of culturemania; a splash of hysteria drowned mankind in common. All feelings were washed into one tide.

Everybody knew it: this crumbling memento to a devoutly dedicated past was doomed. It must be visited in immediate terms of now-or-never. Soon was it due to collapse, like man's own mortal heart and his bag of emptying lung-wind.

The international proliferation of such ecstatic despair brought tourists rushing in like Indian tribes on tracks joining to a mutual warpath. This out-of-season frenzy jumped up the town's treasury booming. The world over, booking agencies were stampeded for tickets; a farewell crusade poured in by boat, plane, car, and train, by bus and by foot, for the sentimental nostalgia of bidding a monument of dead spiritual magic goodby. A single destination was central to a myriad passages. Only the migration of birds can parallel this vast breadth of unanimity.

Itineraries were rapidly rerouted, business timetables suspended, deadlines postponed; vacation schedules were altered, holidays adjusted, for this necessary of all trips. Plans and directions were recharted in one concerted hurry. A mass pilgrimage flowed its relentless flux on this vanishing mecca. Their object would imminently be no more for material eyes.

Babies prematurely leapt to adolescence, just to reach an age that would glimpse the tiniest appreciation of their era's final link with a genuine historic relic. Monks and nuns came with vials for tears, and mimeographed prayer sheets to chant from. Vulgarians and philistines were infected by the culture-rage, and left their bourgeois pursuits of gain to jump on the bohemian bandwagon and come to swoon before this fashionably doomed altar. The publicity image of this homage would advertise and sell in bulk all their crass products and services. Martyr-like sacrifice was bound to boost business through exemplary prestige. From all lands, the well-dressed and those in rags arrived to bloat the tourist rate of a grieving town whose rehearsed mourning concealed tears smiling from fortune's glittering bliss.

Every nation was represented, some by official committees, some by regal visits of state, some by ranking ambassadors, some by busloads and planeloads of clubs, groups, organizations, and schools. Ladies of fashion and the jet set arrived with their entourage. Squads of reporters and photographers came on behalf of communication media. The number of academics and clerics staggered the imagination. Even curious foreign animals managed to swim or climb across, proving that Evolution was enjoying an upswing in cultural participation, even those species designated as low creatures, such as colonies of migratory ants that diligently made the journey with numbers that increased along the way. Fish crawled up the river for a view.

Creeping things and swinging were chartered cheaply on a cut-rate voyage or came with richly endowed luxury. The town was milling with them, exceeding spatial capacity, accommodations, or sanitation. Nobody minded. It was festival time, like a comet's visionary appearance on the sky's lower show window once or twice in a decade of centuries.

There were so many languages there that one would have thought that the declining tower was none other than that of Babel.

The town's mayor and monument's curator were given celebrity status, as befitted their improved standing in the world's gazing eyes. They were subjected to highly flattering television interviews, fawned upon, and lionized out of all restraint. Their autobiographies were serialized by an eminent ghost writer, then translated into all dead or recent languages. They were proclaimed international heroes, and presented with brand new wives, as status symbols or live medals. Their every word (whether an informal utterance or prescribed doctrine) was recorded for posterity's heeding ears, and analyzed with various metaphysical interpretations, according to the most semantically brilliant meanings possible to ascribe.

During all this, sight was not lost of the prime Cause of

this hullabaloo, the religious edifice being chewed up by tragic decay of time's splendid indifference.

Like a Presidential Convention or Coronation or Inauguration, this Celebration was a phenomenon that would spoil a town in the miraculous benignity of pampering.

This modest town was beset by tidal popularity. It became the focal radius for all local cosmic reference. Without abstention, the universe's majestic varieties jumped in, and landed where everybody else was going. Like those minor animals below on wing, fin, gill, fur, or bone, immense stars and distant moons whizzed closer with flapping wind for a favoured spectacular theatrical view of the extravaganza of an old ruin soon to topple and dissolve in particles of smoke.

The journey of the Magi, laden with gifts and awesome offerings, to a humble Nativity stable, was repeated in this hectic tableau, where Modernity consummated its highest spiritual orgasm in the post-Christian era.

It was rumored that the downfall of Religion itself was symbolized in the impending collapse of this antiquated shrine. Then all theology will become a historical figure of obsolescence.

Empirical archaeologists confirmed this view. Scholars and scientists disputed this technical issue, or debated whether indeed the Death of the Spirit of Immortal Man was implicated in the crumbling plaster. Viewpoints were aired from polarities of eccentric extremism that clashed in an ideological imbroglio. Stale ideas were led to this field heaped with fresh slaughter.

Reigning royalties and their courtly pomp honored this supreme occasion. Even the Congress of Vienna was not nearly so gilded with ostentatious splendor.

But the true lover of beauty and worshipper of the past was, as well, abundantly in attendance. Genuinity vied with the sham, in deriving a pleasurable thrill from the circumstance of an ancient monument being gradually eased out of the present. Nothing could be more solemn or grander than that. Temporal drama was being woven, as a passing construction, before spectators who marvelled with well-informed respect for the magnificent significance of the moving stationary vertical procession of a rusty old building about to call it a day by kicking the bucket and giving up the ghost. Souls were stirred, and God Himself was moved.

The latter Supreme Gentleman suspended the arduous tasks of His current labor, putting it aside for a more pressing engagement. His delegates preceded Him, arranging for a Celestial Visit of State, a signal honor conferred on the town whose only boast was this authentic shrine of times gone by. God made ready to descend. In an age nostalgically devout, this memorial now passing away had been consecrated to His Everlasting Glory – a dedication that *these* days were deficient in emulating. Few buildings of modern times paid Him that glowing tribute, on which His reputation was established in our world of men. With worthy resolution, God has to struggle to uphold His own Honor, due to the slackness in the demand for His Sovereign Presence or existential Existence that characterizes this debased decadent age's impious, dissolute indifference to the reputed idea of Deity. In a day when He was out of fashion, God condescended to visit this swollen town for the privilege of watching His monument die.

As for the local Chamber of Commerce, heaven was right now, on the instant. From high, low, far, and near, their beloved town was besieged by visitors fanatic enough to come with bulging wallets. Right and left, good wholesome money was being spent. An orgy of consumption multiplied a town's rallying revenue. Commercial hearts lifted in gratified prayer. Hotels and guest houses, though charging double, were thanked with smiles of deference, so essential was any roof for a sleeping visitor's head. Restaurant and cafeteria prices soared above exorbitant. The food was so lousy that customers varied the trash, after leaving a briefly sampled plate, by ordering a second and equally obnoxious meal. Plaster souvenir models of the town's benign reason for fame were being purchased swifter than a factory production rate goaded by the bonus of overtime incentive. The printing press cranked away non-pause on explanatory catalogues, brochures, and picture postcards representing tinted photographic images of the ageing wonder. Swamped with every-swarming tourists, this place loomed larger than real life. The overflow sprawled with gaping humanity. Tarts didn't have to *solicit* patronage, but were *begged*: the customers chased *them*.

Traditional outlets like prostitution and gambling enjoyed a greatly enhanced custom. The closer to the monument, the more thickly packed the congestion. This dense cultural jungle was a revolutionary event, something almost too legendary to be true.

This modest town's earning power skyrocketed simply astronomically. The concession industry and the pickpocket trade benefited hugely. Miraculous feats of commerce were a daily commonplace. Business surpassed the most prosperous optimism. Records were broken, currency floated like the breath of air. The town fathers exulted. Happiness was acquiring its most impressive definition. It was too much to bear, and sensitive businessmen openly wept in their fever of unbroken joy.

God's glorious bounty of abundance! An impassioned religious fervor was restored in every breast.

For this extremely welcome stampede, indebtedness was owing to what beatific source? All praise was due, in general thanksgiving, to that electrifying rumor of announcement that an important building's fatal days were numbered to some few tragically remaining heart-beats. The Board of Trade computed a boom popping with unprecedented proportions like muscles that conceal an athlete. Greed compelled an attempt to guarantee perpetuity. This was predictably human avarice. The gold and silver was coming in from all foreign directions east south north and west of a well-rounded compass, converging to a magnetic center. *Preserve* that magnetic center, then: that's logical.

Material lust contaminated that town. From within, of course. From outside was where the market moved in. What a pull, what a draw!

The elders of enterprise were seated at the conference table; in attendance were their apprentice juniors.

Should their buckling breadwinner, erected before anybody's ancestral tree sprang up, deteriorate without their allied resistance? Should the communal origin of income go dry and flake off in annihilation? As yet even, it wasn't too late to prevent this major disaster. The magnet of a solvent finance budget had still not come apart. While good fortune had not fallen, every effort must go up to keep it standing. Diseased ancient chemistry will be combatted by modern achievements of scientific ingenuity. The past can only be saved by means of the present.

What's needed right now was obviously the most radical policy of prompt, instantaneous conservation. To this solution must be added a liberal dose of progressively status-quo maintenance of a thing as it already is (or was a month ago, before the foundations were imperilled). Hordes of people are now crowding about the monument. Revenue is exuding from their pockets; spending is protruding from handbags. There's quite an admission charge, in addition to the town's general facilities for purchases on the necessity, luxury, and impulse levels. God Himself donated these people to the town's thriving welfare. All very well, but they must be pushed back. The rescuing crew must get in there, where the flocking is most central, to begin work on salvation of equal magnitude to the Savior's salvation of the fallen apple of man's degenerate soul.

The committee acted, and acted quick. (This wasn't time for shirking amid the cloud-packets of theoretical verbiage.)

Requisitioning funds from salted-away mines supplying storehouse vats of deeply deposited reserves where the town's buried resources of safely invested capital wealth are sealed in secretion against just such an allocation of emergency usage for survival's rare dearness, the executive committee of elders on the Board of Trade went out and did a good job of hiring. They didn't stint as to cost, either. They contracted a crack team of engineering geniuses specializing in preservative restoration of accredited antiquities. These timely and highly-skilled experts were imported one by one from all over the inside of the world — some being summoned from even remoter places, of astral habitation, so angelically merciful was to be their crucial mission in saving tourism from losing a perfect gem. They were hailed as saviors by a grateful public body. Mass prayers were served, to get God on their side, as Foreman-in-Chief. For these special engineers, the possible was the *least* that was expected of them; the *impossible* was the *real* challenge, a test of almost exhilarating difficulty. Nature's decay must be halted by way of a miracle — a *planned* miracle, with blueprint deliberation. Natural law must be opposed to the full, by a constructively enlightened artifice. Art must save art from losing its battle against natural time. It was a task built on classically heroic lines. Only utmost genius was qualified to succeed. Their labor of invaluable salvaging was directed to a very frail edifice indeed. Bending in some dishearteningly gnarled directions, its spiral seams twisted with columnar disintegration in cracks treacherously leaking rot, the structure had a center which somehow wouldn't last out or hold. Ravaged by time, the sagging building swayed like a tender string suspended in a high storm range between parting clouds. Those chemical engineers faced the pressure of having to work quite fast. This project wasn't intended for lazy bones. Look overhead: A circle of vultures swirls in descending spirals, patient for their fell appetite of a plunge. These ugly winged beasts of foul prey scent a soon-to-be corpse of culture to feast on with gruesome glee, grimly chewing up chunks of historical flesh and spewing out as rejects the bones that myth must make its sparse picnic on. Oh, chase the sky clear of these gloomy birds heralding darkness; and may our sun shine on this old temple cleanly new and sound!

The engineering associates had to order their materials from a list of top-notch manufacturers, mindful that the monumental patient of their surgical know-how was plagued with overlayed encrustations of age's ancient burden. They acquired internal beams of durable quality, though at a discount for the product's firm being publicized in this newsworthy venture. They bought steel-tipped nails of sterling precision. Hinges, so oiled that they were slippery, were a further necessary article. Cement advertised to harden any concrete mold, was also ordered, by the can. Since lace curtains were on sale, some fine patterns were acquired for morale-lifting decoration by a somewhat effeminate member of this brilliant engineering combine. Paint was bought, for some good stiff coats to be applied. (The color scheme was worked out by votes, with the result that the harmony was the least offensive to the average esthetic taste of those practical technicians.) Concealed props and wall girders next were lent to the well-buttressed effect of stability that would prevent this creaking temple from caving in. Herculean glue helped to join together some shy individual parts. Insect exterminators were found so useful that a deal for bulk quantity was most economically arranged. Undeciphering ointment was wedged into carved scrawls of dates and initials. Hairpins, candy wrappers, cigarette stubs, and other defacing marks or unsightly blemishes were plucked loose, swept clear, cleansed free. Indentations were filled up. Care for the surface was an investment in depth dividends. Disposed-of details totalled back a recaptured whole. Magnified piecemeal progress was cumulative. Busy haste enforced wise patience in a fussy pile of proven results. So far, so good. These engineers were just what the doctor ordered for a sick building. Moreover, they were the doctor himself. Color floods the monument's cheeks; health stirs. It has relinquished that ghostly pallor. Despair is converted to hope, as a town warms its concern in the flames of a cunningly wrought deed. Matter is submitting to man's masterful brain!

These gifted engineers were hardly idle. They ordered lots of elastic supporters to keep their restored structure from lapsing into an unsightly middle-aged sag. Adhesive devices of tensile strength proved valuable matchmakers between lonely sections of the hallowed edifice; individual panels, so forlorn before, now participated in group relations in an over-all system of therapeutic interplay: to behold it was an inspirational stroke of organizational revelation. The rehabilitation of key areas of this architectural wonderpiece proceeded at perfection's stepped-up pace and steadily monotonous rate. The busy squad of experts took heart with increased zeal of industry, encouraged by each patch of success to the ardor of craftsmanship, work well done as a reward and stimulant for continuation of same. Pride and achievement reinforced each other; how well was the temple being put together! It was conforming to the original shape its inspired builder had had in mind and executed so many centuries distant back along the invisible reverse of time's abstract path! The ancient was newly visible! Art's mighty endurance was holding out!

An architect long long dead was being artistically revitalized! Oh how binding art is! It literally unites man!

Superlative rendering by a past, forgotten architect —

your work entrances today's eyes with modern naive sophistication of admiration!

Your conception bred a form, and the form holds good, containing your conception to the full – it hasn't leaked out!

You imparted life to something, then died yourself. What has survived manifests your spirit yet! It was a *soul* you were fortunate to articulate. It's a soul that hasn't become fashionably dated. You who perished, made what endures! You commanded art, and retain your noble rank. What commotion you cause! Crowds are cheering outside. The engineers are performing a eulogy for the unknown architect who never envisaged what a vulgar age would grow around his masterpiece. The town is banal. Immortal folly is old, new, the same. Another today punctures an indefatigable world.

The engineers are reviving the inanimate old thing, so that it holds firmly. Endless adulation is accorded to them. Their honors multiply, their fame mounts in proportion to the amount of enthusiasm circulating in the combined cavities of all breasts of human diameter!

They *replace* the ancient architect. They either represent him, or really *are* him. Praise is lavished, as their efforts are cheered to completion. They have resurrected beauty! They have dared, in terms of sustained scientific objectivity of realism, to invoke Magic's aid in a feat that incredibly extends restoration's honorable old boundaries. Or so it seems, judging by an overwhelming response by people interested in tourism, commerce, beauty, and other forms of human endeavor, however mundane in versions vulgarized by corruption. (Appreciation these days is conspicuous. But rejoicing occurs to hearts in their *private* capacity, as well.)

Ply on, great engineers! Gallant men, your humane deed shall nobly reward you. Magnitudes of gratitude wait to adorn the success of the bold labor in progress. Don't let go. Surely you're far ahead, you're winning!

But no complacency, just yet! Keep it up, you immortal friends and benefactors of time-invincible beauty!

It won't slip away. You're erecting the thing solid again!

They work with unabated vigor. They employ anything handy, utilize all tools of ordinary household maintenance. They twist screws in where needed. They solder, weld, and meld, with plastic fixatives, standard joints, curative sprays, lime-base mortar, patches of miscellaneous material, from repair kits for the homey mechanic or the thrifty housewife with a spool of thread and her camel's-eye needle. Physics, chemistry, and allied disciplines are referred to; the results are out-standing. Not even a beaver-eyed critic can fault their detailed accuracy. They were paid for the job they're doing so well; they're fulfilling *their* end of the contract. Having taken a complex structure and overhauled it, they allow to take place the reflecting, back to recognition, in a modern mirror, of an antique that connoisseurs had given up on. Surely this accomplishment is not of a small order? More than a semblance of the original has been resuscitated. Were the past still to have eyes, those eyes would behold, against the strange background of a changed world, an image once familiar in early rays to those eyes, and now strikingly refamiliar, a re-creation free from the impediment of transmission. As before, it stands, the monument. The surrounding town and world are different utterly, but here's this object, still taking up the same space. A corner was torn off time, and made consistent to a knot.

Had these engineers resorted to crime for a base career, what immaculate counterfeiters they could have been, or undetected pickpockets, or confidence tricksters of agile facility in the guile of a cunning craft. Instead, they devote their skills in virtue's efficient service, to boost the common good. They're no impotent arm in God's power to help man in his bungling struggles to achieve recognition in the status of a civilized animal.

Toil on, they do. They fuse, repair, spray, connect, smooth out, re-activate, set operative, lacquer, polish, finish, straighten, solidify, turn into joining, impose pattern, correct, convert, alter, rectify, mend, align, reconstruct, round out, clear up, file down, bind fast, tighten, tone down, heighten, lighten, weigh down, secure, liberate, install into place, sweep, comb, pack firm, uncongest, set off, tidy up, deodorize, repel (insects), purify, cleanse, purge, offset, alleviate, compensate, bring forth, materialize, introduce, set up, put back, shift, renovate, re-arrange, replace, spruce up, forge, even out, place into order, beautify, sterilize, unify in effect, free from erosion, render whole, emancipate, make immune to decay, refurbish, knit together, mold into harmony, make radiant, reconcile, conciliate, select, reduce, add, combine, release, harden, lengthen, truncate or curtail, systematize, wrap going, confine, unblemish, awaken, brighten up, unplug, highlight, emphasize, relegate, sacrifice, stress, choose, restore, unleash, restrain, manage, deepen, find, uncover, unfurl, reveal, translate, illustrate, freshen, spring into organization, renew, revise, discover, innovate, improvise, interpret, explain, block out, restrict, suppress, show clearly through, filter, bring into being, make into steadfast durability, actualize, concretize, complete, succeed!

It's done! A transparent lineage to the past!

They came down from the scaffold, and had to enter a file of elongated queue, to be embraced or shaken by the hand. The ordeal of a heroes' reception. Mayor, Curator, elders, proprietors, a Chamber of Commerce in full force, the beaming townsfolk, the entire population itself, committees from all over the world, inspectors, journalists, television hawks, turnouts of opinionated blocs, a mob of tourists, the stalkers of publicity, the exploiters of fanfare: all proffered congratulations in a gruff concord of vulgarity. The religious monument seemed to recede, as the engineers took a primary foremost in the precedence of scope. Second to the sun, their notable blaze fanned the universe.

The town's holy shrine realized a permanent second youth.

Archaeological antiquarians were consulted. They calculated that the restored monument will not merely endure, but prevail as well as survive. The term was fixed somewhere between forever, eternally, and endlessly. Thus, longevity would be no problem, but a blessing of long standing.

It was estimated that a dynastic succession of reliably tireless janitors should be on hand to ensure thorough upkeep. The precious building should never be neglected. History wouldn't have the heart to condone a town's responsibility for the anticlimatic ludicrousness of an ill-timed second collapse. (Even though the first collapse was averted by those dashing young engineers under veteran supervision; they'd scattered now, and all gone home, dragging honors, trophies, medals, wealth, and most-merited conceit in their applauded wake.) Sensation would be too jaded to witness attentively the drawnout crisis of a second threat to the building's impeccable integrity (now established beyond immediate doubt, relaxing tension and soothing scarred nerves).

Precautions should still be taken, as formerly, against natural hazards and unnatural predicaments perilous to the shrine's safety. Demolition bombing would be a destructive eventuality, if advocates of war ever took control. Peace must be maintained at all times; even local outflares should be stamped out and blotted with ashes. Eathquakes must be promptly extinguished, as well as volcanic eruptions belching a coarse digestion from intestinal roots mangled by malcirculation. Hurricanes; forest fires; tornadoes; epidemics; crop failure; spells of black magic; mass misfortune; biblical catastrophes both prophetic and diabolical such as the forecast end of the world and a general uprising of dead spirits to plunder and rape in anarchy's mismanagement; a deluge of baptismal drowning: such phenomena are to be held off, repulsed, and circumvented. Unlikelihoods are to be treated with distrust. Careless habits are to be abolished. A stern prudence will preside over the gift of this building to extensive mankind's growing generations. The renovated structure is expressly intended as art's dowry to a philistine future.

Its safety was snatched from the peril of emergency's teeth. Reinforced now, with pads of protective fat and strips of surface armor (transparent, to allow the beauty to shine through), this cellophane-secured, plastic-covered, cobweb-wrapped feature of any tourist's itinerary bulges vertically erect with erotic pride; stroking the sky, it caresses some virginal clouds accessible to its arching reach of supreme, masculine art.

Listed in guide books as an 'immemorial memorial', it's the focus of paternal attitudes by the relieved town fathers who undertook the expense of its fabulous salvation. These materialistic entrepreneurs proclaim hypocritically that their noble town attraction was restored at high cost to benefit 'posterity': by 'posterity', however, they mean, bluntly, 'prosperity', which *sounds* close enough. Money supersedes art, in their psychological motivation register. They own an interest in a famous shrine for private gain, cashing in on the selling power and surprising commercial pull of something old enough to be ruled as 'cultural' by esthetic historians. This is an acceptable fact. After all, they *live* there.

Their luck doesn't hold out; momentary comfort is dispelled. Some air hisses loose from the secure inflation in their bankbooks. An unforeseen decline takes place, touristically, in that dependent town. This trend scares them, and reverses all previous optimism.

In droves, the tourists stay away! The demand vanishes. Who wants to go and see, from miles abroad, what's permanently accessible now that it's safely restored? It was all the rage for sightseeing fashion when its existence dangled precariously on death's cliff. But that's all over, for the romantic danger has given way to a snug fixture. Why rush to see this relic, when one can afford to take a whole lifetime about it, since the structure was repaired with immortality as its built-in ingredient?

It was bound to outlive any potential tourist; immediacy having lost its lure, and urgency its piquant goad, why not wait, and see other things first? Life goes slowly by, and is long.

Tourists will get around to see it when they're dying – but that's far off.

Other preoccupations were much more compelling. No need to bother breaking a gut to hurry off for the sake of some dull tourist trap that's finished gnawing the dry dog's-bone of its day.

A shroud of voguelessness (like those vultures, now departed, at the time when decay seemed to be winning its internal destruction) encircles our barren relic. It's not even guarded any more, so deeply it's plunged into unpopularity's staunch solitude. No echo can recall those vanished mobs. No sign remains, to indicate the former fame. Only *it* is left behind, unseen by lengthily traveled eyes. Here's time's ignored trophy.

Memory, like art, is but a short song. Undefended by hearty throngs of tourists, this monument is invaded effortlessly by Time's near-by battalions. Abandoned by both its commercial and its art-crazed friends, deserted to the weedy field of fate, this solitary building develops a stooping droop. Rats chase each other in its merry basement.

No new crowds nourish architectural vanity; probe the marks on those vast interior surfaces; explore details subtle to architecture's art; study the uncanny spiritual effect of harmony, decked out in the radiant mysteries of an absolute essence.

The poor town begs for relief. Its country puts it on charity. Red Cross ambulances bring apples and donuts to stave off starvation.

The Mayor and Curator are sent packing to disgrace. Their exile is *imposed*, whereas the other townspeople are *voluntarily* banished. A folk-drained town is soon self-emptied of the humanity born to it.

The bigwigs have gone bankrupt. Unemployment causes a wholesale evacuation. Steadily, the aura of a ghost town replaces what was once a highly-prized stop-off in the wanderings of world-cluttered tourists, for the sake of one gem of monumental architecture.

Occasionally, some visitors still do arrive. But they're only old. (No vendors molest them, since the town is commercially defunct). The feeble and the infirm are the last faithful tourists. Tottering as the shrine itself once did, these ancients hasten to pay, not their last respects to a doomed antique, but a personal visit before the world sees *them* out. They come to see the dismal old ruin not for fear that it will perish, but in the dark conviction that they themselves are the ones doomed, and without engineers to restore them (in a job of salvation-renovation acclaimed for its perfect haste of timely brilliance by a universe that then proceeded to pay no further heed to a safe, newly-painted old bore).

To what's old, only the old come, to wrinkle irony tragically. Perhaps the skeleton crew of the former Chamber of Commerce should build a burial ground behind that bothersome monument, and an old-age home for senior citizens as well, who stray in from abroad with senile veneration for art and set about the laboriously delaying decay of death's mechanical animation. Having come from so far, they wouldn't be able to make it back home again. So here, under the shadow of what was once rotting, and is now bereft of care or preventative treatment, these sleepy travelers would protract their disintegration in a setting suitable to their ceremonious motion into a cemetery's haven of rest.

Otherwise, how could business be revived? No magic halo is sported by that superannuated religious relic. It would not do as a miraculous healing shrine such as Lourdes in France, which has profited exceedingly from the custom of the superstitious of all nations, those hysterically afflicted and sufficiently devout to procure the private benefits of a cure.

Tourism is a highly difficult art. But art is no perfect assurance of a high touristic turnover. Ascertainable predictability lags behind.

The tourist market brutally fluctuates, in its fickle application of fashion to art.

Can a town recoup its losses? Hardly. Its greedy capitalists miscalculated. But they did do one thing: unwittingly, they saved a monument for posterity to conserve. (An international team of restorers is moving in, with the latest in anti-decay devices, to consign the shrine to immortality – again! It's a different engineering unit this time, employed by a World Body for Cultural Preservation. The slumbers of the dying worshippers – those elderly immigrants who camp along the site – will be momentarily arrested; then they'll be left to fall back to the peace of corpsey stillness.)

Posterity, in the long run, won. But *prosperity* for those town leaders in the venerable, brittle art of commerce? – no. They're martyrs, while Art marches on.

THE ART OF CONCEALED ABORTION

Crippled by life's agony, the man sat on his brain for an hour. This more or less smothered several oversized thoughts. When this reverse hatching occurred, only broken eggs remained, like worries with their skulls cracked.

He met a girl, and kissed her through a swift abortion, while they held hands. Working with all their might, they produced a dead life. From then on, their smile tilted to the ugly side.

Then, to forget, he turned artist. He fought against colors, and stabbed the canvas, where muddy blood formed as a protest against meaning. He copied nature, and in retaliation, spring was delayed by a month that year. Then poverty crushed his art, and the crumbled bones formed a neat skeleton where he fell. He looked like a motheaten self-created work of sculpture, and was put on exhibit underground. His girl friend, spry after her abortion, and already bearing the seed for another one, scattered her feminine tears along his anonymous plot. His paintings went for firewood, in the municipal dumping ground. A journal was found. In it, there was evidence of mental deterioration. Its words were clumsy, but had origin in the dictionary, whereas his thoughts and paintings were obscure in their reference, depending on bare ideas of nature and his past.

His girl friend claimed the journal, underlined her own name where mentioned, and, because of her higher education, completed sentences, inserted commas, and rounded out the tragedy. Delayed by her second abortion, the work was completed some time afterward. Through a lucky series of contacts, from lower to higher agent, in which the sale of her love was included, the script became a famous movie, a popular box office hit, and soon there was a stupendous demand for the paintings of its poor subject. Phantom auctions were created, and genuine originals became a fabulous obsession of every art dealer. Hundreds of ghost painters were employed, each representing a different phase of the artist's development. Museums were clamoring for a sample. Art hysteria hit our country, ruining the careers of current artists, looking beyond life for the works of a dead man. The girl friend was now known as his wife, in a posthumous but hasty marriage. A sequel to the first motion picture, by popular demand, projected a great genius into the history of our culture; and stuffy old Europe, with its outmoded art, looked toward these shores for its legendary universal image. The fan clubs were by now international.

The actor who played the hero had to be retired from the screen, to preserve the triumph of his role, and keep the movie ever identified with its subject. There was a movement to kill the actor, and thus have his death comform to the real-life death of its original, linking the actual world with its immense satellite, Hollywood. But the actor, protected by several aliases, slipped into oblivion, and was unrecognized except for his black glasses. He commissioned an art instructor, and is now painting in precisely the mode of the myth-like man he had portrayed.

Meanwhile, a technicality developed. The abortionist threatened to sell his story to the press, unless the great man's wife divorce her dead husband and marry him. The ensuing legal problems, clarifying the fidelity of a widow, freed the woman to marry her abortionist. She then paid to have her new husband sent through medical college, where he graduated as an M.D., much to her pleasure. Then they carefully produced a baby, and it was actually born. They named it in honor of the great man who had brought them together. True, they lived in his shadow, but the shadow was paved with that comfortable substance, wealth. Art had profited, too. Everybody was now imitating a certain artist, and amateur brushes and palettes were in evidence everywhere. Luckily for the human race, the artist had for some reason never mentioned abortion in his journal. Either that, or his girl friend had discreetly attended its removal.

LOVE BY PROXY OF SOLITUDE

Along the journey of reminiscence, Billy-Boy summed up his life so far.

There he was, almost at life's halfway point. Three times, love's arrow had scarred him "permanently"; four times, it had nicked him seriously; seven times, it had nipped him to an outcry of pain. Once, it had been mortal. He'd recover in the depths of death's tomb.

That should be six years ago. Since then, Isabel had been made into a mother twice. Billy-Boy had been superseded by a double-father husband who took marriage institutionally. Isabel was cemented fast beyond reclaim.

Billy-Boy had accomplished an unyielding bachelorhood. For this feat, he was awarded solitude's silver trophy. Despite its heavy burden, he couldn't just shelve it and leave it: he carried it, like an emblem, anywhere he went.

Solitude, in fact, was his identity-label, to a sounder depth than his alliteratively boyish name. Facially, he conformed to that most public role of his privacy.

Girls who otherwise might have been interested in him as a romantic prospect or as affair-fodder sensed the confirmation of his solitude that lopsided him to monolithic predictability; then instinctively, and sensibly, they dismissed any notion of however tentative a bond with him, except as only a "friend." Billy-Boy's humiliation advanced thus to a hardened pattern.

Billy-Boy's childhood could be described as "unhappy." But analysis failed to cure him. The remainder of his life was so molded to fixity, flexibility's parole was futile. He'd remain a "loner." He hadn't touched the pit's bottom, as yet, of loneliness's extremity. Time would facilitate this motion's melancholy goal.

The day gaily belonged to spring. Billy-Boy got momentum into his stride. He walked briskly on the park's side of sprightly oak. Green blossoms showered on him with the fluff of pillow-feathers.

Soon came a slight resumptive of self-pity. Isabel was wheeling a baby carriage, her older little boy keeping pace alongside.

Billy-Boy rapidly shifted his direction. But he'd been sighted by loved eyes prosaically unloving.

Distance couldn't blunt her shout. "Come over," the voice beckoned, like a bomb's casual descent.

Weeks of agony waited to follow this one confrontation. Billy-Boy quickly escaped, running headlong into his own embarrassment, that wore Isabel's staring face.

He moved to another apartment, at the contrary end of this city's populous persecution. Emptiness he needed, not such a sad fullness.

Lacking its solaces, Love was for Billy-Boy the one be-all for life's full bag of drama. Love's inner soul was romantic, and its outer body consisted of sensation's bond of clinched embrace. He sought love at dancing halls, dinner parties, cocktail parties, art gallery openings, the deep-groined vault of gray mausoleum-like museums, casual park pick-ups, theatre or concert-hall intermissions, late-night bohemian bacchanals, the magic of momentary meetings, contrived offhand introductions; and by any legal method, however it made dignity sag under the embarrassment of need's clumsy gigantism. Sometimes he'd light upon a sex affair, or a fumbling chaste flirtation: but these were armored with an impersonal character, a stylistic mechanical formalism of nondescript consequence. His solitude remained evenly in place, like a coolly combed head of hair unruffled by a pretentiously endearing wind.

Unexpectedly, a girl named Sue fell for him. All Billy-

Boy had to do was reciprocate, and he'd rid himself of solitude's oafish virginity.

He tried to be impressed by her most attractive qualities; but with all the good will in the world, Billy-Boy was not smitten; he contrived to deify her charms, but only succeeded in observing their multiple imperfections. He suffered: his Solitude was immaculately out of reach: even to a girl who in turn suffered in not bridging it to hers, allying two banks in an arc of love's throbbing flow.

Sue wept; at the other end of this telephone hook-up, Billy-Boy responded with all the aloof indifference of an inaccessible mountain peak. Their end had come. Sobbing her life to the winds, Sue replaced the receiver, gently closing out Billy-Boy from hope's dearness and the dream's farewell promise.

Billy-Boy was free; costing the token tithe of pain, his solitude was unscathed; it could resume its tragic career, in its slow gradual road to misery. The threat of being detoured by Sue had been averted. Solitude's interior star would now sing its destined dirge, a solo mournful to the heavens. How agreeable was self-administered sadness! Billy-Boy's warmth was most pleasantly chilled. Autumnally, the splendor of gilt foliage thickened his flaming veins with a wild outpour of grief. (In the true world, Spring was spinning a hazy beam to scaffold July's majestic height.)

Sue was invited to dinner by some friends. Isabel and her husband were co-guests. This is how Sue, jilted only recently by Billy-Boy, met Isabel, who six years ago was for Billy-Boy the one sorrowful love in his life, the central jewel in solitude's sterling work of craftsmanship. Having rejected him, Isabel was thus ably qualified (once Sue had confided in her) to advise Sue how to go about winning Billy-Boy. Her role as an amateur psychologist would now serve Cupid's solemn mission, to relieve Billy-Boy of his gloomy robes of bachelorhood, and assist Sue to reverse her recent forlorn misfortune.

"He *ought* to get married: he's over thirty now, and he just mopes most of the time. (That's the report I get about him: we still have some acquaintances in common.) He's between jobs, and is lazy about getting ahead. He's a brooding introvert. The other day I was going by the park with my children. He was around the corner, I saw him between tree trunks. I did what was only natural. I called out to him, because six years were passed, he had time to get over me and not be so emotional. But then, of all things crazy to imagine: Lingering love gave him a cowardly fit, he vanished deliberately out of sight! It's obvious that he still hasn't grown up. There's only one way for him to mature: he needs someone like you. This is where you come in, to round out his complete personality. The way he's been going is waste, ruin, tragedy. Sue, together we must save him! He's worth our combined effort. If you seduce him into loving you, he'll get over that obsession about having a lonely complex. The trouble is, he *suspects* any romantic interest in him; he thinks he's so inferior, that he couldn't possibly be loved! So if he *is* loved, he regards it as an intrusion on the solitude he holds so dearly to, like a lifebelt in an alien sea. The time he and I went together, I learned a lot about him. I didn't choose to apply it for my personal advantage in forming an alliance with him, but now it's for you to inherit the benefits! But first, assure me that you really sincerely want him!"

"I do, believe me! − provided my case isn't absolutely hopeless! The way you described him bothers me − convince me not to doubt! − can he possibly change?"

"Only if *you* stick fast with real insistence on getting him. *He's* so defeatist, *you* mustn't be so, by giving up too early or on some easy note of discouragement. You've got to *work* to win this sticky character, this tricky, slippery guy with the built-in self-sadness system! What a wild customer, if you can haul him up!"

"All right, you sold me. What's the first step? I guess I'll have to phone him."

"No. The trick is to force him into phoning *you*."

"But how? He seemed so cold to me. He wanted no part of love. He was pretty definite about it."

"There are ways. Just wait. Come to dinner tomorrow. By then, I'll have an infallible plan. Foolproof, you'll see!"

"You *are* a dear. Never could I repay you − never!"

"Don't try – it's no sacrifice. I'd be a very happy woman to see you two merge together: *he*'d benefit, and you'd be an incomparable pair. I have an inspired intuition that it's true! This project so excites me, I'm wet! If we can only pull this wonderful thing off! That's what creativity means!"

"Sorry, I'm still disturbed by one thing: If he thinks himself so unworthy of being loved, mustn't he think me even *more* unworthy, to be the fool to take the pain to love him? If he turned me down before, how am I any different now that he shouldn't spurn me again? – I know it sounds distressing."

"Your outlook is wrong – get rid of that pessimism! Now, here's our address: seven-thirty tomorrow night. Just trust in the constructive ability of my plan!"

"But Isabel – he doesn't even care for me physically! I'm not his type! I have no appeal for him!"

"*Force* yourself to take a more positive attitude. You think that by being negative, you're being realistic! You fool, Sue – I'm sick!"

"I just couldn't stand being hurt a second time – it would be so many times worse! Oh, I'm sorry you're angry! I submit to your counsel. I'm in your hands: Direct me!"

"But smile, silly! Lift up that droop on your pathetic face – you look so dubious, I'm afraid to operate!"

To conceal the woeful cast of a face with out-of-control features, Sue placed that face inside the sloped hollow of Isabel's shoulder. Hidden abashed in smother, she embraced this person who still possessed the long-lost dark Heart of fragile Billy-Boy. That heart scorned by one, desired by the other. Perhaps a transfusion, a transference, would lodge that wrested prize in the ample nest of Sue's tender but spurned bosom. There, the heart would be tended to so delicately, nurtured at the fount of affection's deep solicitude, that it would grow content in the mating sanctuary of delight's permanent address! Yet Sue felt ugly, in those neurotic pools of eyes behind which, in a swamp, was the abandoned hut of Billy-Boy's self-critical soul. Sue's stunt – her dedication, in fact – was to explore the sullen wilderness there, and discover some civilized outlet for the purity crippled in repression. Sue would open up his song of loneliness, and graft it melting onto hers. Their tears will waft them to the open transport of a union. Signed in rhapsody by their attending angel!

The following night, Isabel presided as a female sage. After dinner, her husband left the room so her talk with Sue would nest securely in that frankness afforded only by privacy. Billy-Boy's character was analyzed wide open.

An outspoken intimacy fell upon the two women. Billy-Boy's heart was openly transferred from the knowing bosom of the one (ending six years of quite ignored residence) to the trembling, unconfident, eagerly rent-free breast of the new nominee landlady. By instilling hope in her disciple, Isabel had doubled the force of Sue's love, whose resurrection made Easter's Ascension seem like a short jump infinitely below the gothic rafter in divinity's steeple.

Never had Billy-Boy been loved so. It even pierced his oblivion. Though he was now at the other end of their city, Sue's passion charged almost to his ears. The vibration whirred so hard, the defense alarm clanged like a lunatic. A general conscription was called, as Solitude's manpower was recruited from reserves of a slumberingly standing army. Bugles blared out the creeping closer of danger's crawling demon. Not the welcome Isabel, but the dirty daring of an infidel.

"So I'll phone him myself," volunteered Isabel, disclosing her cunning solution. "I'll invite him to forget me, and then be my friend. He'll visit me platonically, and I'll plant seeds with your name on them, in that weedy garden he calls his heart. From me to you will go his displaced love. He won't wait, but rush out of my house and phone you alone with secret trembling. You can expect a proposal, once the decent interval passes. My life's great thrill will come to fruit! Sue, you happy bride already! Kiss me, your smart savior!" They embraced violently. Their plot would have no trouble succeeding. The air stirred, to the twin throb of the bleating feminine heart. Billy-Boy's fate had been rectified. The guarantee was as dandy as a lace bonnet. And not so quaintly outmoded, either.

No sooner had the telephone been installed in his new apartment, but it rang promptly for Billy-Boy. He alertly pounced on it: the call, a most radical factor, altered his life. Love's own voice was saying, "Let's be friends."

"Isabel, will you renounce your husband?"

"Silly boy! Of course I love him! Come right over for a drink. I have some news to tell you."

"What news?"

"Not now – come!"

"But the subway would take an hour! But you want to see me! Say no more. I can understand. I care for you enormously! Be still till I arrive."

Billy-Boy suspected that Isabel had fallen tired of her husband; that belatedly, it had wisely dawned on her to heed True Love. What a joy was that subway ride! He had won a passive triumph after all! Happiness rode on deception's flying horse. Illusion's wings felt so solid, that by sensation's law they *must* be true!

Like a homeward hero returning from a Victory of State, Billy-Boy flew up the stoop to buzz open the door to claim outfrustrated Love. But only Isabel's husband answered. After reciprocal introduction, Billy-Boy was ushered in – by the very man he would ideally design to cuckold! Isabel was still busy with the children.

The husband and he made "conversation." This polite murder of awkward time forestalled the dishonesty of sincerity. The visitor's sole goal was to take possession of a love withheld to the exile of six years of suffered isolation. After all that, he finally had the right to be impatient. Imprisoned to interminable patience and the tragic suspension of hope for so long, now he longed for outright release. To slake thirst, and fling aside torment, at the bold, raped immediacy to force open Isabel's lips! Even to the husband's view: for one must lose to let the newcomer win. And the newcomer had been first, before. Now he arrived to find what had only been lost. To restore the world's balance, and even out time's odds in the jilt of delay. Prime's former season was summoned from the dead. Ripeness earns a second chance. Let jubilation escort it home.

This conspicuous pause bulged in an agony of bigness: Isabel's awaited appearance had not materialized to release the instant. The husband's dull presence became opaque. A transcendant hush looked past him. Billy-Boy slighted this overcome usurper's immaterial existence.

(The slight was noticed and stored away for a future flare of resentment. The husband suspected an unconventional tension, and shrewdly guessed its cause. But he feigned innocence, with a business speculator's guile.)

Now Billy-Boy must succeed his successor, to wrench the stolen prize of vengeance from the smug possession of its legal thief. Excusing himself, the husband left Billy-Boy to contemplate in expert solitude the restoration of justice in the scales of divine hunger's metaphysics. The next tableau called for Isabel as an original substitute for anticipation's flickering projection of an ideal picture. The re-assertion of reality's sceptre, not its impressive shadow. To solidify the emergent dream, and be love's individual symbol. In this mental way, Billy-Boy spent emotional minutes regarding Isabel at the shrine of portentous image.

"But I'm thinking of *Sue*; For*get* me; don't ever hold out hope again. Really, you're so immature! It's in*cred*ible that you don't appreciate her! She's not really bad-looking, in fact she's a dear! You'd find her more adorable with the years. Really, stop crying! You're a grown man!

"Oh, stop that now! You look so miserable — and all for me?! I tell you, only *Sue* can console you. She's worth ten me's. I can't rival her little finger even. My husband and I are well matched (all our friends tell us that); but *you* and *Sue!*: an un*beat*able pair! You don't know what's good for you! She's a marvel! *Phone* her; — you're too upset. Here, use *this* handkerchief now. This is the most unmasculine exhibition I've ever seen! But don't worry, Sue will never know: it's only *our* secret.

"Here's her number — should I dial it for you? Your fingers look too helpless to do *any*thing! Oh, come, don't start that sobbing again! Your breast is heaving like a hurricane! This is too comical! Oh, ha, it's ludicrous! Ah — .''

Isabel was stifled with laughter. The hysterical peals rose to mockery's shrill emulation. Mortified, Billy-Boy waited for her heaving to subside. But *his* sides heaved, letting his sobs ease with spasmodic control.

"Yes Sue, I really *would* like to see you. Yes, I *want* to. I've just been speaking to Isabel. She's fond of you, she's a good friend. She was just praising you. No, I'm not there now. I'm in a phone booth. Sure, I want to visit you. Get ready — I'm coming over now. Not enough notice?! For*get* your hair and your bath. I'm not interested in them. I got to see *you*."

They became engaged. Once things had begun to get rolling, Isabel shrewdly left town, having arranged to have her husband's vacation take place then. It was a critical point in the game. Her absence would force a singleminded independence on the genuineness of Billy-Boy's affection for Sue, unaided by Isabel as a scheming prop. Billy-Boy fell back on himself — and forward onto Sue. Habit had substituted Sue, assisted by pleasure, for Isabel, in love's interchangeably romantic plasticity. Sue even *dressed* like Isabel, and did her hair the same way. And Billy-Boy, at first, *wanted* to be fooled. Only self-deception blocked the violent entry of some irrational act.

Isabel's perfume lingered on Sue's person. Sue was all of Isabel that he could have.

Being obedient to Isabel, he was able to possess her in his eyes-shut embrace of her otherwise unattractive intermediary. It was as directly far as he could get with Isabel, by carrying out her summons to its utmost letter. Kissing her delegate meant being warmed remotely by the real thing. For a poet at heart, that would *almost* suffice. There was a superficial benefit, as well: the curse of physical abstinence had been lifted. (But on this point, the spirit also cashed in:) It made vivid the Isabel he idolized. Indulging his carnal sense cleaned a purer clarity for love's lofty abstraction of Isabel. Purged was the worshipper, as the shrine glowed more heavenly.

Sue was stoical, in fortitude against knowledge. Sensing her secondary role, she restrained despair and played a waiting game:

in time, Billy-Boy was hoped to identify, then substitute, the symbol for the thing it symbolized. The symbol would *become* the Isabel who, being unattainable, would dwindle to a fluttered vague dimness: she'd merge with the Great Memory, and be in particular forgotten. Sue it was who would remain, as the emblem or trophy turned concrete. Or else, as the soiled oasis; the shallow dregs of consolation's worn-through mirage.

Isabel's husband had to return to work. With him and their little boys, Isabel came back home. Billy-Boy lost no time in phoning. "I want to submit my progress-report to you," he whined aggressively. "I've been making headway with Sue, you'll be glad to know. Why haven't you communicated with us? We're officially engaged, I can tell you. Didn't our letters get forwarded to you? You place yourself out of reach of our gratitude. That's unfair, for someone who was so responsible. Can you get away from the children, and meet us for a reunion? That wasn't graceful, to do a disappearing act. We owe you so much, it's a duty you shouldn't want to escape from. We would have tracked you down!"

"Yes, you 'owe me so much'! — but do you owe me this threat as well?" Isabel retorted like a roused prey. "That's what it sounds like, with your voice in that ugly tone. All right. I'm sorry, then. But I want to see the both of you *together*. And come *here*, where I can control it. Now, down to cases. Are you serious about getting married?"

"Deathly. There's no question of disappointing you."

"That's nice. But for her own sake?"

"Of course. Sue's the only girl I ever loved."

"Don't be funny, it's rude. Don't tamper with emotions; they're too delicate for your gross trifling. I'd hate you if you hurt her."

"Then you won't hate me. I'm bound, the issue is settled."

"Did you fix a date?"

"Sure, but it's indefinite."

"I'm not in the mood for your humor. Will you both come to dinner tomorrow night?"

"How can you be refused? We've taken your word *before*."

"I told you, stop being cynical. Then I'll expect you at eight o'clock. I'll be glad to see you both. Till then, give my love to Sue."

"But not to me, eh?"

Isabel said goodby for politeness, to seem gradual about hanging up. She became worried, and regretted her interference. It had been no little passing whim in his phone voice, but some stark defiance that transgressed civility and suggested an animal baring fang with raised claw. A survival of the jungle primitive was behind his witty banter. Its foreboding had a grim chill.

Much more tangibly derived was the uncertainty that *Sue* was subjected to. Matters had become unpleasant. Billy-Boy had treated her unkindly. A subtle malice, like a kind of slimy ooze, had seeped out, or trickled forth, from some of his ambivalent "cracks." He hadn't paid her a single respectful love-tribute at whose core was devotion's eloquent courtship. His cavalier dismissal of her human status was cruel to the edge of monotony. Pretense at being engaged had been laughed away. Only his sexual pleasure had been unfaked. No, that was wrong — nothing else had been faked, either. Not the slightest hint of romance, except in irony's form of manifest insult. Sue was no Isabel-substitute. That rang clear. The indignity! Her starved dignity would need to be re-asserted, not fed with irony's rotten crust! Rebellion swelled up with bristling burrs, in her chest of despised femininity that had been debased to a cesspool for lust's casual inspection. Decency was on demand by her outraged personal humanity. Billy-Boy would have to supply it, or Isabel atone.

"Come along, don't get difficult. I love you, so let's go. Isabel expects us both. My reputation isn't sneaky. She won't like it, if you don't show up too."

"*She* not like it! I don't mean to sabotage your infatuation, but what about caring how *I* feel?"

"Look, I *know* how you feel. Meanwhile, I happen to be concentrating on her just now."

"What for? To drag her into adultery — isn't that what you're using me for?"

Billy-Boy kicked Sue swiftly on the shinbone; a display of electric sparks umbrella'ed from the pain. Sue submitted, as her principles were gagged numb.

They arrived, like an ordinary, close couple. Isabel received them guardedly. Her husband suppressed annoyance. He was fed up with Isabel's glamorous role of deceit and intrigue. He resented being left out, and yet wanted to keep his nose clean. Sue was sullen and subdued. A blow-up was brewing in her, but no advance rumbles betrayed it, except the discontent that was clearly exposed. The eating had begun. Billy-Boy's eyes were bright, glowering with mirth or mischief. Isabel studied his face with furtive glances. She detected in it a desperation, a defiance, a hatred, and an insolent daredevil cockiness. She foresaw the possibility of physical danger. Billy-Boy was a bad loser: and he had lost *her*. Vanity first might chafe, but then the protest would be blown to a storm's vehemence. She must apply her power tactfully, to keep Billy-Boy in hand. She must outplay the wrath eruptive in his spirit of cutthroat revolt. She must contain this venom, keep the aggression from spreading its sour spew of pus along this path strewn with other involved lives. She must regulate, conserve, defend.

Coffee was concluded. Sue's bitterness discharged the first volley. Strident with wounded ingratitude, she let go on Isabel a nasty catapult of accusation. The husband was amused, and grateful: his wife's interference, or "assistance," was construed in the light of a punishable offense: the others would do the incriminating for him; he would sit back, in silent righteousness, to observe her destruction; she'd be put in her place, repent, and be contrite. She'd be a sweet wife, and learn submission. (And not dictate when their vacations were to take place. And not make him amicable to unruly guests chosen in her own machinations.)

Billy-Boy gallantly defended Isabel's honor with such a rude crack, Sue recoiled like a snake semi-sliced with a hacker. Then, for further instinctual preservation, she ducked in retreat behind a timely barrage of tears. She was drenched sopping dry, taking desolate refuge behind the barrier of grief's lonely deluge. The storm pattered out her dirge.

Sue was out of it for a while. Isabel scolded Billy-Boy for his vicious assault on Sue. He protested that he had punished Sue for attacking Isabel. The hostess held up a hand, and requested peace. This was reasonable, for those strained circumstances. The husband was pleased, and smug.

Billy-Boy was cordially hated from three sides. Sue felt betrayed by her lover and her helper. Isabel felt ganged up on; her husband had assented, while the couple she had experimented with were popping shots at her. Bad feelings had infested the dinner. First appetite then digestion, were poorly provided for, in violation of harmonious hygiene. Rancor and recrimination abounded.

That husband enjoyed silent immunity. He had his spokesmen. He was a tacit partner in the persecution ring that had Isabel in a shuffling trap. She was angry and scared. She had contrived a mating bridge between lonely hearts; but it snapped back with recoiling springs, sprung cables, elastic girders, to react on its surprised but kindly intentioned engineer. The project had collapsed; the blueprint had miscalculated, with an architect's fantasy. And what right had her husband, to join the jeering conspiracy?

She had match-made, by rubbing a combustible couple together; the conflagration had caught fire, to scorch the igniter. The husband wasn't even singed, but he would fan the blaze. Inflamed passions easily take perverse turns. Or bake some worse burns. Isabel was a martyr, a stake consumed to ash. Her plan had shed only heat, but little light.

An hour after dinner, the blacklash of misfired purpose was still tearing spiteful gashes in the bitten-down, chewed-up pulp of Isabel's battered pride. Four people were glued together. They remained at table; the table united their discord in a central square of cloth-covered wooden neutrality. Wine fed further flares to common dissension. Aggravation grumbled like a hound injured by rebuke. A sprite bellowing curses had the run of the room. Misshapen Evil crept in to have a look. Insult brooded; its tongue spilled out of its mouth like a boiling pot of poison. Forces were at work; supernatural smiths hammered weapons for doom's last ditch. Wicked colors stultified the light. Four souls stuck it out. The ceiling crumbled, and hissing smoke entered the room. A black cloud with ugly contours scraped the quartet. It was not laden with cherub-strung harps and pleasure's sonorous instruments. Strife chased the tail of Disorder; while Anarchy, indolently lounging, ate lizards by the gulpful. Only the husband wasn't keenly suffering. But even on *his* brow, tranquility's sweat refused to streak. Monsters were being spawned left and right, with no respect to pedigree, precedence, or natural law. They took over, while human perspective receded with safe faintness. Roars and hallucinations danced in mathematical chorus, heedless of orthodox phenomena. Revelation struck the four principal figures — but the bolt rebounded, to drive a spike through the Devil's gaping foot. He retaliated by crucifying the cosmos, including measureless eons of space. Results are delayed, by several light years.

But the husband swore by nothing but realism. Imagination had taken the upper hand, so he retired in good order, with unruffled poise and a smirk of pity for unruly children, from the wild upheaval in the room. The embattled trio were left to concentrate their turbulent dissipation. Repressions were flung aside, as having no place in the proceedings. Sue's target, in abundant glee, was Isabel. Billy-Boy chose the same victim, and was ready to resort to violence as the appropriate technique. Ganged up on, Isabel consulted her wits, but they were out of order. Disloyalty surrounded her, even from herself. Control and assurance had run astray, leaving her in bare distress. What reason could she argue with? The arena was not mental. Logic would not halt gladiators on the circling dust. The used plates on the dinner table could not reflect a wholesome scene. Emotion's naked body, bruised with dripping glands, was obscenely on view. The cups and silverware had a dull luster. Isabel gambled a leaping step.

She blustered into the air, piercingly: "Get married, both of you!" she commanded, resorting to authority's ruse, hoping to recall the habit of obedience in her one-time wards now posing as graduate opponents in combative play. Rays of grudge replied; and dissent's barbed wire, behind which hostility's hardware of snouts was poked with unblinking clanks. Isabel reached for a fork, but was intercepted by a counterthrust. A loving hand molested her fundamental right of motion, and was intent on inhibiting other freedoms as well. Six repressed years clamped down.

Her wrist whitened in Billy-Boy's grip; to this bone-breaking pressure, he added severe corkscrew twists to vary the harmonic dissonance in pain's trills, runs, trebles, and rife muted effects: she herself was the vocalist, and in tune with the instruments she deafened the hall with a memorable scream, operatically among the higher registers. This retrieved her husband, who heeded the call and came racing in. He broke the marauder's grip and shoved him flying to a corner, where a bystanding lamp flickered, fell, but played down the drama by not breaking in the thunderous crash. All those involved were stunned; momentarily, arrested motion produced the momentous apparition of a pause. Indrawn breaths poured themselves out, to mingle balanced components in the air's stricken flow. The moving film was stilled to a solitary photograph. The grouping of the figures centered on a dynamically offset composition, full of the pomp of pose in the quick of heat, caught in the supreme moment of unconsciousness. The snapshot stirred; then sequence, regaining lifelike speed, overtook the arty hesitancy.

Sue's revenge on both Billy-Boy and Isabel was being carried out by themselves on each other as though by mutual defeat, in deference to her armless wish. Seeing her passive will granted by her victims in pendulum orgy of roughhouse affliction (assisted by the husband's intervention as a countervailing measure), Sue fluctuated between those two polar guilts of Grief and Relief in doses of alternating potency or in opposing currents of resisted emotional completeness. This conflict drew her in, and sprayed her with diffused mysticism. Her simplicity was colored in complicated tonalities. She'd be immersed in a bath, splash around a bit to remove the external coatings and foreign coloration, and get out of the tub as a woman again, her skin rippling with consistent pores. But now, agonized ecstasy quite wore her apart.

The husband took over. It was his house. Isabel froze to a corner, shrunken and broken up. To re-establish order where riot had roosted, the husband banished that pair ludicrously mismatched by his fool of a wife. They stumbled out, in dragging disarray. The husband beamed. Victory was his, over the bohemian insurrection; his sensible mind had prevailed, as the final word in an undefined dispute. He was the master. Isabel nursed her wrist. She appealed for his forgiveness. An .erotic impulse surged and tingled in him. He seduced his wife, forgetting that he was her husband. The pleasure on this particular occasion exceeded the usual and hurtled past the ordinary. Her dangling wrist introduced a kind of fetish. But it was the unsettling disturbance, that little local riotous turmoil he had just stamped out, so upsetting to regularity, which had raised his sexual flame to its relishing zest of delight. He was the strong man, to protect his wife.

He had rescued her, and proved supremacy. Now she must request, not demand. He, it was he, who was the man.

While the peacemaker exulted and resumed command over a household exorcised from spells of perilous ordeal, the estranged but bound couple whom he had deported to an ignominious exile floundered in midnight anonymity in the dark city's barren streets. Their state was not tidy. Demoralized with the tipsy syrup of corruption, they wandered with no fixed goal. Gruff and grouchy, Billy-Boy made an indecent proposition, repugnant to Sue's dishonored virtue. She had already been more than sufficiently compromised. They embarked on a scolding session, until Billy-Boy tried to force the argument with such strongarm tactics as that from which Isabel was only now recovering (following a marital bout of sorts and kinds). Sue was manhandled, pummeled about, given ferocious wallops, in his writhing grip. In reflex, she kicked his shin; the jolt echoed to his coils; his flailing hold slackened, letting her slip away in an awful coupling of terror tangled with remorse. Her wounds bore bruised nerves. Love had been trampled underfoot, as a creature too lowly to be revived. Pain was compelling perfect sense. Like a torpedo, realization ripped its trail loose under the canopy of collapsing sails. It resolved her, like an oracle. No more would she submit her sordid, morbid vulnerability to a madman's whim. She was quits of the whole deal. Anguish and shock had curtailed her career as a dupe. Some other man would find her attractive – a man gentle, kind and normal. She would pretend love, and live out the cheat convincingly. The acting would turn it true; a sounder foundation would uphold it. Not a remarkable fate, but better than being cudgeled in a brutish honesty of passion to Billy-Boy's exciting range of anti-institutional strangles. What was he snorting rebellion against? Isabel had made her aversion clear. Sue would carry her compassion elsewhere; she'd clear a path for a fresher victim to volunteer. Or for Isabel to be crushed, in case Billy-Boy's business there has an account of unsated vengeance, from an appetite too conscientious to be replete. Isabel had a husband to protect her from undesired love that was too stubborn to die. Sue would seek one too, for shelter from exploitation and cruelty; and for values on a more affirmative scale, which experience would construct a rationale for, in her course of growing together with him. Any dance would yield dozens of prospects. Instinct would pluck the most likely candidate.

For forever, Sue stepped down from his life. Isabel, as well, was given the privilege of never hearing from her any more. The grotesque triangle was stripped of a corner. Disaster had rubbed away *Sue*'s angle, leaving one corner empty, of that odd triangle of contrary wills. One knot had come apart: the interlocking was unraveled by this notch. Like a worm truncated by a third, the organism might coil itself to some strange endurance, in its twisting life left. With one corner eliminated, two still stood as the rushing tournament narrowed: One avoiding all contest, the other to push aggression beyond limits tolerable to society's tribunal of conservative decorum. An arrow guides this one-sided clash. The reluctance of the one is countered by increased violence on Billy-Boy's propelled part, as the loser forging rugged compensation on an oppressed victor.

He loves her. Impossible to moderate what can't be helped, either in fury or extent. Love rejected becomes hate – big, bitter, and complete. It's so excruciating, desperation's rule of all-out war, without recourse to pity, is invoked. Restrictions relaxed. Anything goes, when belligerence motivates anarchy to get going. He'll raid her house, ravish her by force. So what if it's anti-social? Such scruples don't deter true individualism. What's the prospect, from here? Anger versus defense, with panic thrown in to the latter. Husband away working all day: field is clear for rough maneuvering. Victim ought to cringe. She's lost that initiative she once enjoyed by virtue of domination as Cupid's agent. She's so scared of publicity, she fails to ask for police protection. Target easy, must be toyed with first. Set sights, employ power, inflict maximum suffering. No dainty concessions made by war. The conditions are too special, the delights too cruel.

Billy-Boy stalks, with rashness nobly proportioned. Enemy too frightened to inform husband. Stalker lurks in alley, peers in at screen, spies at street angles. Free all day to harass her gradually: between jobs, drawing government compensation. Put it to good use. Unified purpose, not squandered in dreaming. Action, to test results. Enemy knows she's trapped. Barricades herself in; her kids weep: it's summer, they want to go out to play. Billy-Boy would hold them for ransom. He has unlimited funds of immorality to draw from.

Billy-Boy total barbarian? Not one civilized spot left on his inner surface, where humane appeal might softly blandish this decent good man gone criminally astray? Open to whisper of love's quiet reason, cooling rampage of love's sour fever? He's on a haunting vigil outside Isabel's prison. A reluctantly bereft ghost, he's a reincarnated plague, a moaning idol of evil grief. A gruesome mask, to kindle demonic rituals. Spell hovers over tense Isabel. In her, a civilized anxiety in fright against archetype savage. Deep fear of basic primitive: In self, or externalized. Billy-Boy becomes figure, myth — representing dark forces. Oh, eliminate him! Husband, husband, why can't I tell you?

"Don't worry. I have my own hunches. I can smell a rat when he leaves his dirty scent. I'll take care of him. I'll make sure he won't bother you any more. Leave it to your husband. I know what's up."

Her husband was too reliable not to suspect foul play. Tenderly, but firmly, he questioned her. Like a dentist extracting a wisdom tooth, he extracted her difficult truth. Bloody root and all. Billy-Boy was on the loose. Have to pin him down, not easy to handle. Can't placate an unreasoning man with reasoning means. Fight him on his own irrational ground. Tame a savage beast – not by music, either. Deal him straight, man to man. First enlist some trusty friends – plain, solid, strong men, upstanding in this neighborhood. Fellows who not only can tell what's right, but go out and *fight* for it.

These uncomplaining citizens of convention's unofficial army help a husband to set an ambush trap to catch a maniac who's hot bent on raping a helpless wife. They get him, too. Rough him up in a simple, straightforward manner, to teach him to associate punishment with an intention that's plainly wrong. Then a little more, too, by knocking him out of commission, reduce the potency of his threat. Now wife and kiddies need not fear, but go out to shop or play without the least unpleasant second thought. Normal human rights, set back at liberty, and ahead to progress.

The culprit was really done in. Out. His body a pulp, and his head squashed of thought. Some bones misdirected from natural course. He's in sad shape, a sorry specimen.

It's early morning. Garbage collectors on their routes of mercy. Angels of sanitation.

They sweep up Billy-Boy, send for an ambulance, and watch that human refuge be carted away to the nursely attendance at a hospital sanctuary. By the capable professional skills of whose practitioners he'll be set going on the recovery shift. To be dumped out on the conveyer belt looking like an artificially new model for second-hand consumption. That's lovable Billy-Boy, in his process of bony rehabilitation, skull and all. Just a few carved interior corrections.

Convalescence needs comforting. Visions of Isabel penetrate his medicinal stupor. She floats by, regroups, filters in shades, is formed anew, reverses direction, appearing simultaneously from many places, in a multi-spectacle, like a pageantry of clouds in richly shifted contour. She's his visiting angel, companion in constancy. He, the connoisseur of solitude in that black art's most dissipated refinements, assimilates dreams of Isabel for his huge mental sky's flux of weather. He revives, he's well again — approximately. He's released from the merciful hospital. It cured him of being beaten up. He *looks* all right. But what's inside?

He packs up Isabel in his bulky luggage of material imagery, and sets delicate foot on the humming city street. He's free to decide: should he seek a new city, or keep living here in his apartment? His first timid reflex advised in a stern old man's tone, "Leave! It's no good for you here." But his own voice got the last word: "Don't go away! *Stay*, while Isabel is so conveniently here."

But his anger's insane pulse has died. He wouldn't actually accost Isabel again, or stalk her purposefully. A memory clicked, warning him not to.

He develops his grand aptitude for dreams. Sitting on a park bench, he meditates. He hasn't gone home yet. His luggage is beside him. He has the faculty of depicting Isabel "visually" in poses of stupendous immodesty; the cunning vixen has enthralled him. Rapturously, he gazes through his haze.

Dusk swoops down, closing the park. He's turned out at the gate.

The subway home. Everything as he left it. Small apartment, untidy. His. No concealed spy. Enchanted by his ribald visions of Isabel, he surrenders himself to a coarse indulgence: the grandeurs of infantile self-abuse, undertaken with rigor and disapproval. Isabel is "there," like a succubus. Silken veils slip away, her thighs shake their smooth undulations, a dazzling creamy thing to behold. Suddenly she admonishes him, snapping a stern finger and lisping some slippery words on a tempting, tiny tongue, to the total effect of: "You adorable naughty!" He sobs with joy and fatigue. The room compresses them both tight together. His coyly bold mistress, whose charms have no sum of calculation except in the strict rule of infinity (whose code is yet mortally undeciphered), distracts him incessantly. (From what? From not thinking about her.) She casts a seductive benediction on him. She soothes him into the beautific surf of foamy calm. She bends over him, magic dropping from her breasts like phials of perfumed potion.

They kiss an eternity, as the clock averts its handless face.

Clutching at his animal root, or its tattered stub, its weary stump, he's wafted aloft on slumber's steed, and set down in a gorgeous palace. Here repose languors, clad skimpily.

He's granted an audience with Queen Isabel, in a chamber deeply recessed, hidden in a maze of erotic corridors. There she is, on a stunning throne. Kneeling on knees of crunched bone to be blessed by this haughty regal apparition — this real, prepossessing beauty — he sinks through a trap door disguised among the gold mosaic tiles that embroider the majestic floor. His fall continues into a far depth. Snugly settled inside earth, he's walled in by a sealed shelter. But the dungeon has holes for breath. Seemingly buried there, he yet possesses all comforts and necessities for life's gay round of amusement, though restricted by his *solitary* captivity. He's even equipped with the latest spiritual gadgets. He lacks nothing, except company. Empirically, he's quite alone.

But contemplation has other ideas. Embalmed in the mysticism of meditation, he conjures Isabel's shade: she joins their underground love nest. Now he has her: she's trapped! They'll die or live *together*. She's *here*, with *him!* Love's prisoner, forever.

Only one qualm remains: She's a goddess, and he's only mortal. But Union *thrives* on inequality. Only miracles (whose age is over) can quite sever them. So Billy-Boy has won his prize. She's the most shapely Solitude he ever had.

WHAT MARVIN CARRIES

Marvin was always afraid of losing things, so he packed them together in a big black bag. He was *still* afraid of losing things, so much so that he didn't trust the big black bag, despite it being sealed tight and containing all those things so organizationally at once.

So he put the big black bag into a larger valise. He still feared, so he stuck the valise into a suitcase and locked the suitcase. All that luggage should afford him the sense of protection. But his insecurity prevented that. For, what container should he wrap his *insecurity* in? None, so it wrapped *him* up. It carries him, he's conveyed, he's all the things he fears to lose.

THE IMPERISHABLE CONTAINER OF ALL CURRENT PASTS

I discover, in my girl, layers and layers of mineral deposits, archaeological strata from her encounters with previous men. These physically encumber my right of entry, and I ask her why she collects such outworn trophies. She sighs, and says, "I venerate the past. It has such masculine endurance."

"All fine and well," I agree, "but it impedes me. See, I'm left in the cold. How can I force my way in?" "Push harder," she suggests. But ah, so many things in the way! They thwart my active principle, and I say, "I'll remain outside, where the space is cleared of insurmountable obstacles." "Very well," she agrees, and extracts from her shrine a sample of the accumulated debris, which she examines with both hands. "That was Harry," she says, sighing with fond remembrance. How loyal she is to the ghastly vigor of traditional emblems kept forever in her museum of private erotica! Yet, at all hours, she's open to the public. The crowd is uncontrolable, and traffic regulations must be put into effect. Coming and going pedestrians stumble upon the remnants of their timeless ancestors, in her legend of impure, but popular, precedence.

The clutter doesn't discourage visitors. They leave their calling cards, and are filed in that amazing perservative. She's a conservatory, where the past bulges with immense lingerings. Additions are daily recorded, to stagger an impotent future. The world overfills itself, and teems with fertile overgrowth. She's due for an internal cleansing, to sweep clear the dated and admit the endless present. Let her restore her storage to the flow of successive newness. Then movement is possible, and a vital avenue of penetration.

"Try again," she implores. I strain, and then plunge into the dizzy totality of historical disorder; it's like building a housing project on a monumental cemetery whose inhabitants, according to the latest fossil explorations, belong bonily to each epoch of retreating phases raging to the evolutionary source itself, when living forms, squirming out of mud, oozed at the sight of my girl and first settled into her ample beginnings, which were to accommodate, in her mania for collecting, all subsequent species.

I'm the latest, but by no means the last. She ages only into an enlarged youth: the capacious wholeness of her widening warehouse is that interior female to unlimited containment. Nothing, once in, goes out whole again; and what remains is for the ages.

One day, my girl started bleeding at a place upon which I had sexual designs. In order to exact poetic justice, I then so beat her as to make her bleed in areas outside of the erotic zone —wherever those might be found. Thus, I neutralized the sex drive, and brutality proved to be my tranquil compensation. When the blood-letting had terminated, I was properly appeased, so much so that sleep found me a not difficult customer. Meanwhile, my pleasant victim whined so softly, that I was carefully undisturbed. Her caution was thus wisely at the disposal of an unconscious desire to survive. Which proves that she's too selfish to love me in the ultimately self-destructive sense. This, in turn, justifies the beatings I'm forced to adminster on her all-absorbing body. Her soul, I can't get at; psychological warfare is one of my weakest points of attack. Therefore, I merely abuse her in the physical sense, as a direct expression of my means of honesty. I'm admired by my girl for being free of sneaky devices. If it's contact she wants, where can she find a dealer less apt to be deterred by scruples of the slim skin?

Just when I caught a cold, my girl sprayed a blunt portion of perfume on each and every zone of that topographically mapped principality of her primarily erotic republic. (So I wasn't provoked, my nostrils being stuffed up.)

She didn't know I couldn't breathe. "Can you scent a message?" she requested. "Not I," I replied, letting innocence be stupidity's tactful diplomat.

"Can't you whiff my signal?" she asked, while hay fever pollens used my nose as a rush hour subway station. "No, why?" I said, letting naivete act as a spokesman for innocence, who was already engaged on another wire.

"Can you sniff what I have to send?" she implied. The meaning failed to reach me, as well as those deliberate fumes. Ignorance had been delegated by stupidity, innocence, and naivete to be the practical administrator of their fouled-up functions. I'm wearing perfume," she declared.

"I don't see it," I answered: "can you show me where?"

"It's here, simple," she pointed out, discarding her clothes to permit clarity a finer show of brevity.

Not even asthma could make me allergic to my tactile formation of enlightenment. Substituting touch for smell's unruly sense, I wound up with the same goal.

LUGUBRIOSITY

I

(Stage is bathed in faded light.)

When did you die?

Last year, around May. When did *you* die?

Just the other day. Tuesday, I think.

No *wonder* you look so fresh and preserved!

Not for long. Soon I'll be developing that ghostly pallor.

Yes but it will *become* you most appropriately, considering where we are.

Oh, are you always looking on the bright side of things?

Sure. Since there's no sun here, I've got to make my own *artificial* one.

But there's a *worried* expression on your face.

Oh, that's because I forgot to turn the light off before I died.

What light?

The electric bulb in the bedroom. I'm compulsively fussy, because every time I switch off a light I cut down on my electricity bill.

(Aside:) He doesn't know, even now, that he can't take 'it' with him! *(Aloud:)* But surely a doctor or a relative must have switched it off by now, or else a landlord will have done it for you?

I'd be most obliged to the one who *did* do it, *if* he did it, but I have no way of telling, because there's no postal delivery of letters to be received here, and the telephone is blank, it never seems to work.

Yes, we *are* cut off. I feel *out* of things now. I just don't seem to be able to keep up with things like I used to.

But that's hardly *your* fault, since you can't help it.

You're pardoning me on the basis of fatalism, but I myself believe in free will.

Believe in it if you want, but it'll do you no good here.

Well, then it's an *abstract* belief, or a principle. Not all my ideas are for expedience.

Anyway, somebody must surely have shut it off by now.

Shut what off?

The light. — Don't you remember?

No. Illuminate me.

II
(Darkened stage.)

We're in the dark.

(Boastfully:) Not with *my* knowledge.

Why? What is it that you know?

Everything — you name it.

Where have you left your modesty?

Modesty is only typical of *life*. When I died, I left it behind.

Is there anything *else* you forgot to bring here?

My wife. She's remarried recently.

How do you know? We receive no news.

Intuition tells me.

And I guess you knew her long enough to make an educated prediction about her?

III
(Neutral, or dead, stage.)

Haven't you got any life left in your bones?

Life!? *What* bones?!

Those things inside, that keep your skin pinned together. .

Skin!? Do you see any skin?

No, but I don't see God either, and I take *Him* on faith.

(Aside:) That's the only way you *can* take Him. *(Aloud:)* Have you only become naive *since* you died, or were you that way before?

I had a lot of practice being naive in life, because my naivety was up against a whole wordly *world*, which helped to bring it out by the emphasis of contrast. But *here*, where there's no *world* as a background for my naivety, my naivety is pale to vanishing, like white on white.

(Scornfully:) I never thought of death's atmosphere as being particularly naive.

Well, it's not *worldly*, is it?

No.

So you agree with me?

Why not? If our *bodies* are in the same fix, let our minds be as well.

Bodies! Did you mention bodies?

Why, is that a sin?

Mentioning them isn't, but *they* are sin.

Sin-ce when?

Since birth. But not now, because we don't have any (body).

(Scanning himself with head lowered. Bewildered, lost tone:) But these are my *feet*, here are my *hands*.

Never mind that. *(Emphatically:)* Did you *die*, or *not*?

I *died* all right.

I don't care whether you died *all right* or *all wrong*. *(Patiently:)* You *died*, and you're *dead*?

That's right.

(Aside:) There's nothing right about it. It's terrible, if you ask me. *(Aloud:)* Then your body's *useless*! You might as well not have it!

Then what am I *doing* with it, then?

That's *your* business. You carted your luggage here, that's why.

But you seem to think it's excess baggage.

Only because you brought it to the wrong place.

But I took a one-way, not a round-trip, ticket.

Of *course*! What do you *expect*? A *miracle*?

IV
(A totally dead stage.)

(Looking bored:) In death, there's lots of time on my hands.
Then here's soap and water: go wash your hands!
Then I might disappear *altogether*!
Then stop complaining about time.
Oh, it's not time *itself* that I mind: it's just that there's so *much*
of it!
It's just your ennui: you're not *active* enough.
But what is there to *do* here?
I don't know. Death is an idle industry.
Plenty of leisure —
But no leisure *activity*.
Oh, we'll rot.
We already *did* that. How do you think we *got* here?
Oh, stop harping back! You're always harping back!
(Offended:) Who's *harping*?! *(Indignantly:)* I'm not an angel in
heaven!
(Ignoring that:) But you're not content with your current fate!
What's so *current* about my fate? It looks endless.
Yes. We may not have been immortal, but we sure are *eternal*!
You're always looking at things from the broad, *general* point
of view.
Why not? It's *serene* that way.
You're just too lazy to go in for *details*.
Details!? Can you point out one *detail here*?
You — you're a detail.
Me!? I don't *exist*!
Oh, don't be modest.
But it's *true*.
All right. Have it your own way.
It's not my way — I didn't *choose* it: it *is*.
You mean it's unavoidable?
Inevitable!
Eternal, as well?
All that.
Then you're not needed. Go back to sleep.

V
(Aftermath.)

Oh, but it's so *sterile* to be dead!
Good! That means we won't catch cold! Good-by!

THE ROOM AS MY OUTWARD:
ME AS THE ROOM'S INWARD

Bottled paper, cartons of running water, boxes of human interest, vats of invisible pins, cans of cleanly laundered textiles, envelopes of monumental balls, and other well-assorted receptacles, littered the cluttered warehouse of treasury-repository, a windowed room with walls between; said windows vacantly staring in on the assembly of misformed objects ill-fitted by motley shells. Somewhere among all this stock, a mirror commented vertically on the scattered proceedings of this interior wealth of still life. From object to object crept a progression of dust, to color uniformly grey this indescribable variety. Intervals of unkempt space thus alleviated the monotonously irregular solidity. The clock's hour of night or day made only the most elementary difference. This kingdom of matter (ranged in slovenly gradations) invited that most human of diseases, Sloth. I personified this sordid vice, for this room was occupied by me in a term of residence. Never had nature and surroundings enjoyed a snugger fit. All that the room was, was but the outward of me; such was the suitability of environment to man.

There was no room for my bed at the horizontal rate of expansion, so it stood tilting vertically upwards at the acute angle of discomfort, creating stoical difficulty for the intended union of sleep with the sleeper: this made my insomnia legitimate by propping it with immediate cause; wakefulness was prolonged in one continuous dreary spell.

When summer sang its lyrical tune (as a favor for spring's promise to itself), I let in the generous outdoors by opening the combined enormity of my windows. The wind blew the dust about. Astray in disorder rippled my papers. Stale untidiness was provided with a whiff of fresh multiplication, while chaos kept up its honest appearance. I was so tired, death yawned with boredom waiting for life's painful slow dullness to complete its midway phase on the uneven descent of a rocket's vital efforts to consume the clowning of its described orbit on the turnings dictated by a cycle. But air was invigorating, and I was tormented by an ache of health. Even a career, in a profession accredited by society, was not beyond the upsurge of my momentary resolution. But soon, so exemplary an intention subsided most dismally, and with a thud I declined to the shallow depths where torpor sustained me with its mud, as vegetables subsist on their diet of foul and consistent ooze.

The door knocked, and Joe came by. Joe's my friend who always tries to reform me. With his misguided goodwill, and his misplaced common sense, he's sure a foil to my intelligent negation of life's well-meant futilities.

"Spruce up, Ira," he calls, a drop from the ocean of his good nature; "this mess is no way to live; it's indecent, and shows no self-respect for yourself."

"Oh Joe, go 'way," I say, shrugging to confirm my point. "It's useless," I added, a phrase from which affirmation was gloomed out in advance. "Try!" Joe pleaded. "No," I moaned, an effortless dirge.

"Oh Ira," Joe said, in tears: "your ability makes a graver disappointment in that your dormant talents sulk in the corruption of their latent forces and the putrefaction of what was once so glowing in promise: what waste," he wailed, his voice dropping beads of oil in oozing scales from pores of populous tragedy. "Grip yourself; be a new man," he counselled, applying wisdom where result stood in an arid festering of its own sterility. "It's hopeless," I appealed, soothing Joe with gentle doses from my limitless fund of apathy. But they were blows – heavy, relentless, crushing – on his hand of proffered kindness, the palm extended, warped now in the frustration of its tenderness. Weeping in the overflowing of compassion, Joe acted a passive Christ for my benefit. I had fallen, so he submitted to a mental crucifixion on some suburban telephone pole, exposed to the predatory nibbling by hawks and passing crows. Nor did I board the ark to salvation, graced as I was by not a tithe of faith in Joe's meddling in my spirit nestling in the sunken harbor of its disgrace, caught conservatively by an anchor's rotting permanence. "Here's a dollar," Joe said, flapping it on a floating current. Then he ducked out, having cursed me with the force-feeding of that green mercenary gift.

Barely has my loneliness resumed possession of me when a second visitor rustles her skirt across the threshold. She's Janet, a pleasant sort of girl were it not for the accidental aberration that's bound her attachment to me by an irrational jolt of bourgeois logic. Her father doesn't consider me eligible; her rebellion against parental firmness thrust her lax choice to my favor, in ties of what devout romantics call love. So now I'm seized on fixed waves of sizzle down to the plunging nest where my embraced corpse must lodge, doing its dance like a doll jerked on puppet spasms to simulate the unvarying pattern known as pleasure. And these were the heights life was devised for!

Our performance had dried itself out, and the distaste of my lapsed appetite now hustled her in clothes and out my very private door, leaving me the soiled peace for my thoughts to coagulate. For recreation, I seized a book. I read some disjointed pages to separate plot from sense and isolate both in a barren tide of mystery outside the choice ken of my selective void known as incuriosity. Boredom gripped me, and bore me aloft as its most reliable child. I emitted so cave-like a yawn, my mouth held open house to entertain some vagrant germs then loitering in my room like tramps of no fixed abode and even less driving ambition. The germs set up a colony down my facial channels, peppering my lungs with potions of poison. I voided my disapproval with a testy cough, but by now the germs were solidly entrenched as guests of no uncertain leave. To warm themselves, they blocked each nostril against the annoying intrusion of draughts. Snug in their fortifications, they dug in, snugly ballasted off for my cold's interior duration. Nor were they rustled by my slightest sneeze; and like vampires, they drank intoxicating draughts from the pitched tent of my fever, in whose consoling warmth they sprawled like drunken dissolutes, tanned by a Miami-manufactured sun in shades of rejoicing purple. As they thrived, I weakened, materially all but defeated. Thus was an official nurse called in, accompanied by an architect. And my room was remade as a hospital ward, disinfected with limp whiteness. My objects were shrunken — all those boxes and bottles and vials, tubes, and cartons — to create space for my recuperation. The dust was carted away, and hygiene installed as a function of architectural rehabilitation, to which I, reclining, was a victim faint with transparent mortality. The windows admitted what sky the city was permitted by real estate hawks. In that sky entered a sun. As I hallucinated, I read much scriptural wisdom in the sun's rotund face. Such wisdom was facetiously misapplied, in my case.

As I was taxed back to health, the nurse lost her undertaker complexion, to be taken in marriage as life's bright wife when spotted wearing only nature's cosmetic as a glossy powder that disguised the artifice under which her identity labored with puffed contrivings. Curing me with healing herbs and restorative balms, she ascended to angelic divinity, leaving an autographed halo behind as evidence of a reward neatly earned. The architect was gone, so my room reverted to normal, a peg for confusion's hat and a night's merciful lodging as an inn for wearied disorder to drop dead with sleep. Now was my rut made refamiliar, and identity restored for recognition at once to identify. And I was old Ira, digging a trench for the gay burial of youth's dwindling memory. Achievement was at hand: room and I blended, and distinction evaporated between the self I was and the room in which that self could view its surroundings. My soul and the room's soul joined mutual factors of nonentity, toward what end only inertia would solve, combating mortal mobility with a leading struggle.

WHAT MARTIN DID ABOUT NOT LIKING HIS NAME

Martin, you look excited, but with unpleasant results.

I have a perturbed announcement to make.

Rid your system of it: Like a cancer ball that the surgeons lift bodily from our cut-open house of stomach juices.

What I have to tell is not as disgusting as the comparison you applied to it. It's simply that I hate being Martin, though I wish personally to go on living. I wish Martin were someone else, even though I had to go nameless for it. Somehow, Martin doesn't describe me, and doesn't even begin to do me the justice of my full self-expression. Can you understand that I'm much more than 'Martin' would imply?

But 'Martin' is only the sum associative force of all your attributes. 'Martin' means different things, depending on which person it labels. There are Martins in this world who are completely different from you. Why use your name as your scapegoat for your general dissatisfaction with your particular abhored life which you must always tediously lead? Your discontent is not a *nominal* matter, but is in the manner of a discord between you and your very life. Your having been named 'Edward' could not have averted this basic disagreeable condition. So give up blaming your name. Try to repair what's *really* wrong.

My spirit is afflicted with malaise. What deeds must I alter, in personality correction, character rehabilitation, identity therapy, to be a person improved over what 'Martin' has come to signify?

Irving is my own name, so I'm hardly in a position to advise you.

I can't be reconciled to my 'Martin' me. After death, I hope to be born again as a girl named Janet.

I wish you success and an early marriage in your next metamorphosis. But do you expect your soul to be the same?

'Martin' *is* my soul. So, emphatically, no.

I thought your *body* was named Martin.

Martin is my characteristic facial feature, reflecting my Martinian soul.

Then you're Martin through and through?

Such is what it seems I am.

Then I'm correct in addressing you 'Martin'?

Yes, that's my local address, which I carry with me, like a turtle with its house on its back.

Then you ought to feel at home, being Martin.

It's my most incurable state of being.

Then you must learn to *live* with it.

Why can't I quietly live it *down*?

That would be self-defeating.

But mortification is good for the humility.

Too much of it despoils the pride.

By definition, I'm very *un*proud to be *Martin*.

How you do castigate, and persecute, your good name!

It's not an honorary title like 'Lord' or 'Duke.' Nor does it even identify my profession.

Yet you profess to be at odds with all that Martin is?

I'm determined to depart from that impediment of an appendage. Yet how it clings, and I'm called by it, barefaced, to my shame, by friend and foe, who have my name in common as an insult to term me by, slurring my reputation and consigning me to the appellation of my infamy. Martin is my disease. Were I to wear a normal suit of health, then 'Martin' would be disused, like the defunct name of a newly coined street. Destiny hounds every man; and for a nemesis, *I* have a name. Like a leper's spots, or a zebra's stripes, or an orator's distinguishing voice, or the mole on a French mistress, or the scar on a wanted criminal's face, or a birthmark that satisfies the morgue's autopsical morbidity, or the telltale colors easily spotted by birdwatchers as characteristic of that species of wingdom be it jay, robin, hawk, or a painted kite. Or an author's style. My name is a dead giveaway for me. It adds not an iota to our vast historical body of multi-classified occult sciences that drill a hole through real appearances and concrete exteriors to reduce the core to a matter of the utmost metaphysics and ultimate consideration, the legend and myth of spiritual entity, on a footing of the absolute, the pure soul of essence. I declare myself beyond Martin.

Well, Martin, thanks for saying so. I'm no more than Irving, but for me it suffices. As Irving I exist. Death will confer namelessness upon me. That's a type of immortality despicable for any ego to contemplate, any normal, self-respecting ego-consciousness worthy of its own integrity. That's why I make much of being Irving *now*, while the joyride lasts of having the self for a property under the stamp of a name as part of its equipment. I don't wish to *transcend* 'Irving': I wish to bring it out with full power. Is a name a handy labor-saving device, bandied about with promiscuous circulation as practically a public ownership? I value mine. 'Irving' goes beyond appearances, and certifies the apparent in its inmost potential. In all justice, I wear my name proudly. Yours is like a fallen flag, like a slattern's tattered depravity of a skirt slipped down to the dishonored mast's ugly ankle bone. Thus drags 'Martin' to a hideous abuse.

While 'Irving' dignifies as it signifies?

I keep my name up, and keep myself up to it. Like a gardener caring for his flowers, tendering them with gentle love's skillful fingers, so that their species will go unsullied.

You wax sentimental, in your botanical fashion, with a dash of inaccuracy to further soil your unrooted premise and sag it to seed in your groundless argument of a mythic garden plot. I got your *nominal* drift, but certainly your reference of words and terms were straying weeds to the wind. I got the impression that 'Irving' means a lot to you.

It does, for I'm *it*.

You'd defend it as the vocal of your own self, evocative of all that your life may invoke to your property-protective mind of proprietorial propriety to the letter of your nominative spirit?

As is proper. Nor is my name a mere prop. My name has become me.

You *look* like Irving; and you *are*!

I don't need your mocking. For you've betrayed the legacy in *your* name. You've let yourself down, and made 'Martin' muddy.

'Martin' muddied me at birth, when I was christened it!

What a blatantly transparent excuse! *You* are the degradation of 'Martin,' who otherwise would have remained neutral and left it for you to prove your worth on its own intrinsic terms. You're a disgrace to whatever 'Martin' could have been, in the signal failure you've made of yourself in bungling 'Martin's opportunity. We've defined, finally, what 'Martin' is.

I reject your definition, as unkind, inaccurate, assassinative, unfair, and highly unflattering. I pronounce 'Martin' to be what I *wish* to be; and from now on, will embark on a dream life, of grandeur and ideals, that uphold necessary illusions that restore pride which life's accomplishments fall short of in the right and entitlement to qualities confirmed by attainment.

Am I below *esteeming* you? — or is that too great or soon a privilege?

I'll allow you that, in time. I'll bestow. Irving is as much below Martin, as Martin is above Irving. That's the scale of my hierarchy.

We're not exactly peers?

Hardly. That's my point.

Pardon my denseness.

THE MONDAY RHETORIC OF THE LOVE CLUB

The members of the Love Club congregate. First it used to be called the Male Club, that being the sex of all of its members. They would tell each other tales about their women, so love became the prime topic of conversation. That's how the name changed.

At each session, a different member relates an adventure. It could be pure fantasy, the mere reporting of a romantic image. Literal coarseness, in general, is discouraged. The tendency is to poeticize love, to rarify its distilled essence. A standard of sensitivity protects the exclusiveness of the club.

A code of regulations constitutes the rules of discipline. Each speaker is granted a courteous asylum against listener interruption. Thus the patient components of the audience are themselves secured, for protocol will protect each speaker when his turn comes. The solidarity of the group is the best assurance as to the sanctity of the individual, so long as he remains a part of the group. Monday night is their meeting time, fresh after the material compiled in an erotic weekend. No wives or girl friends are permitted to attend; women are barred, the better to be talked about. Behind their backsides, much may be revealed.

Anonymity clads the identity of each member. Some know others in the business community or as private friends; but in the sacred clubroom, they're as if masked. A pledge of secrecy and confidence, bound by initiation rites, is never violated, or the member would be expelled. Enforcement is rigidly kept strict, and freedom is banned as being ultra lax.

There's a secretary there, to collect minutes. The chairman observes democratic procedure; and the president presides, the principal officer in the ranks of staff maintenance of order. In case of a tie, votes are decisive. This purges the atmosphere of a foul taint of politics. Honesty is conducted, on the honor plan. This system is aboveboard, and plainly open. Periodically, it's inspected for flaws.

The members are of all ages, a joint nonarithmetical brotherhood oblivious to time differences. Some members have just raised their first pubic hair, while others can't even raise their member any more. From infancy to senility, inclusive, the Love Club is well stocked with American males. What they have in common is the love of women: which, ironically, is the source of what's *un*common. They deviate into particular cases and examples of individual specific uniqueness. When such experiences are *told*, they generally belong to the club at large, as common property. Thus, when each member speaks, he shares what happened to him with his fellows, and the whole assembly undergoes an enrichment, an expansion of its intricate totality. What one speaker says is, such is the unity of the club, magnified indefinitely to astounding infinitudes of depth, such are the multiple variations throughout the magnitudes of an extensive organization. Membership is partially unlimited, subject to due restrictions. The moderator beats his gavel, the meeting is called to order. The minutes from the last session are briefly given, as a spur to continuity: sequences must serve to connect these successive Mondays. Last week, the topic had been the loneliness and indecisiveness of a kiss. The discussion afterward, with its uninhibited release of questions and answers, had wound up in an agreement that the least a kiss can do is to have a girl dangling at the other end; otherwise, the raw and refined material is not there to work with. Hearty laughter had approved of this resolution, whereupon beers and cheers were served up. A spirit of unfeigned mirth had prevailed at the evening's successful termination. Comradeship was plentiful and was generously handed around in a flowing contagion of distribution. Now it's tonight, and a hush greets the speaker. The lights are dimmed, to control mood. Only he who has the floor is standing, on the raised slope of a platform. After an introductory cough (as an inducement of formality), he reveals the course of an affair of the heart: how it began and ended with only himself. A girl had participated, as well. Here's a tape recording, giving his exact inflections:

"I gave myself a kiss, as an act of betrothal. It didn't work, though, because a girl wasn't present to consummate it. I paged her, yelling her name, which floated into the endless wind, without dying out. 'Myself alone,' I said, 'will never do.' This seemed philosophical at first, until practicality used it to its own end. Feeling exploited, and without tangible reward, I gave myself flirtatious airs, and wooed a one-time woman on a sound basis aboard a floating bed, where, back and forth, we swayed to the tides of motion, without quite moving an inch. 'It was fun,' she declared, after it became convenient for her own body to pour speech upon her tiny tongue. Overcome, I fell in love. I was the heart of animated passion, and in a tropical frenzy my ardor was thrust without mercy into the snatch of her sweat. All this was to the good. We even smiled, after first thinking about it. Proving, upon reflection, that even we were also human, and agonizingly so. When it was over, and the romance soured, we became nostalgia's property, and have our memories to thank."

A polite splattering of well-intentioned applause acknowledges the speaker's efforts at communicating a message. He blushes, and then comes the question period. He parries each thrust, and is allowed to escape unwounded. Suddenly, a swelling wave of boredom rises, and crashes on the speaker's head. Mercifully, the meeting is adjourned, and the members retire home early. An epidemic of yawns sweeps over them, and other marked symptoms that betray an evident lack of enthusiasm. As Mondays go, this night was not especially memorable, except as a peculiar specimen of dullness. Next week had better revive a lagging interest, or the club might be faced with an absentee panic. Good attendance was necessary for morale. The trouble seemed to be that the past had spoiled the present, with a bolder tradition of speeches. Newness got successively paler, in comparison with precedence. Should shock effects and standard-debasing sensationalism be carted out, and resorted to as popular stimulants? How revolting to the tenets of good taste and a superior measure of breeding! Compromises were in their very nature abject.

The newest of all their Mondays arrived, up to date. It was the latest current Monday they had ever known.

In keeping with the rules of continuity, the speaker for the evening retained kisses and loneliness as a subject bound to the last lecture. The talk he'd deliver, however, conspicuously lacked a woman as an actual recipient of his well-developed lust. It was a shocking omission.

The moral seemed to be that lips were insufficient, by themselves, as carnal objects of love. Desire is very exacting, in its enormous greediness.

"I had a kiss to spend, and bought a pair of lips. (Not mine, because I'm not for sale. Only now and then.) With those hired lips, whether rented or purchased, which I merely owned or leased, I squeezed out perfection into my kiss, until, as modesty withdrew, lust called in the extravagant body, with its poison terrors gleaming from the criminal dark, but only her lips were there, and intolerable emptiness below. What savage music, and I moaned. Oh, I groaned. And only lips, for spend, or hire. The tiny puritan lips, those chaste emblems of virginity and trembling mock adventures of adolescence, so puny in the size of my passion, and the depth of my thrust. Ah, my seed. Where is your fertilizing mother, the wicked measure of my pleasure? Hidden, flirtatiously concealed, lost in the stroke of absence, where darkness and light don't mix. There I can't see her, and yet, gigantic imagination creates her monstrously complete form, while my emotion sags and delivers, free from its obsession. What have I wrought? And only lips began, where sharply sin shall climax. And guilt frowns, the mouth hideous with blood."

When the speaker had concluded, silence stirred its trembling vibrations in waves of soundlessness within the hall's four broad walls. Collectively, the audience shook its one multiheaded head, as a gesture of mass dissent. What did it all mean? That a kiss wasn't enough? Any fool knew that!

Then arguments heated up, and fumes of cigars poured forth. Scattered groups conducted informal debates on ambiguous topics, based on the uncertain value of the kiss. A kiss had a decorative utility, but not a meat-and-potatoes role, maintained some die-hearts. Women needed a little more substance, seemed to be the consensus; and men themselves found finer joy in blunter instruments than the lips sported on their barbaric faces, under which hair grew if not shaved. Kids can kiss, but true adults try their lick below, where the game assumed big-league proportions, at mature risks. Each member of the Love Club privately bestowed on his own tool a heartfelt blessing, with fondest wishes for a continued uplift of fortune, an extension of its spotted career. Each tool responded with a glow of joy, in a true magnetic current.

Thus the members were united in a general swelling. The hour struck late, so they said goodnight, adding, "It was swell." They went home under a heady steam of stimulation. Their wives or girl friends received a pleasant surprise, but soon found out that a kiss was not the end it was the means for. Grunts and pants ended the evening.

Passion weakened into a week. Time so turned that another Monday came pop out into the present, giving a rounded approximation of its next appearance, propped on a newly erected reality to release the power of its potential in pulsating clarity. The scheduled speaker had prepared an amusing talk, the narration of an endless kiss. It was to be a long and complicated speech, in which a third party was to be introduced, as an addition to the usual first-person male and his girl friend. Cobwebs were cleaned away from concentration, for this mental obstacle endurance hurdle marathon, told as a secondhand sporting event in verbal images. The subject was a kiss protracted to an unusual length, and its morbid consequences. The tale begins in the hospital, where the speaker and his girl friend are held together by lips that can't be tugged apart, a kiss that physicians are trying to sever. An old friend of the speaker calls up on the telephone to find out what happened; he offers useless advice at the beginning, until the speaker is forced to explain, under physical difficulty, how he allowed his girl friend to gain so close an advance on his affections. The effect is highly comical.

The audience suspends breath. Smiles light up the darkness, in spurts of gaudy imagination. The situation is so improbable that realism takes an enforced holiday, and only what remains is described. It taxes credulity, at marvelous interest rate. The coin of attention, then, is promptly paid.

"I felt at loose ends so I looked for a kiss. Such was my innocent intention.

"Loneliness drove me on, in my pursuit of a kiss. I craved its essential glories of contact.

"My search for a kiss ended, but success was too final. I found one, with a suitable girl attached. Trouble was, she stayed attached. That's what brought me to the hospital, stuck to the girl by our lips, and my next problem is to talk over the telephone, where my friend is waiting at the other end of the wire. That's decent of him, but my lips have to talk sideways, with my girl hanging on desperately to every word as though it were the product of her own gluey mouth, grown indistinguishable from mine. Is she eavesdropping, or am I? Hold on – here's my friend's free tripping voice coming over.

"'Kisses are meant to be enjoyed,' my friend philosophized. I was answering him from the Incurable Ward, where my girl friend and I, by spending the night together, were making all sorts of rules helpless, as well as difficult to obey. 'Kissing I know about,' I tried to say. The operator interrupted. She wanted another dime in her box, or else a big nickel. My friend accommodated, falling for her, and we kept on going. 'Tell me your kissing history,' he begged. 'I see you're stuck on the subject,' I said, 'but if it's curious, this is up to date: *My Last Big Kiss*.' Then the operator hushed, and began listening. Her silence seemed like a big woman. So to my collective audience, including a participant where the words issued, I recited, on the top of my wavering breath, to the depth of my lingering death:

"'Kissing always passionately involves me, and it's hard to get a word in edgewise. Once in the middle of a kiss my partner stole my mouth but I was keeping hers in security, so we kissed and made up. It took a long time. I began with three cavities, and ended with false teeth. The only thing we ate was a tongue sandwich, washed down with nice hot saliva. Thanks to my mask, nothing grotesque was born. Were we in love? No, but we gave lip service to it.

"'The fun stopped when her gums had their period. I got drunk being a vampire, but the Red Cross pump-leeched a free donation off me, which broke my girl's heart when I went into circulation. Just one last farewell kiss stood in the way. It's still going on, and we've been transferred to an oxygen tent. Breath gets scarce, and they've grafted our lungs together. With our dying breath, we may vow love. At this very moment, our kiss is beginning to waver. The lips are ready to come off. Flesh has begun to convert to spirit.'

"'Hello, are you still there?' I asked the telephone. 'Of course I am,' my friend answered, 'and I want you to stop kissing right now. It's ruining your health, not to mention other things. Now come off it.' So he hung up, but I was still hung up over my kiss. 'Gosh, you're awfully kissable,' I told my twin. 'I can't help it,' she answered, and kept on kissing me. 'God, I'm losing my manhood,' I tried to say, but was too kissed to say it. How that girl can kiss! The operator must be jealous by now. But the phone was disconnected, and a technician is applying oxygen to it. Could she have fainted? Meanwhile, my girl is pressed close. I'm about to commit myself: but only for a cure. I'll make a miracle-working statement, and the results should release us, since consequences are affected sentimentally by motions of the heart, even if feigned, and love locks any key. Or unkeys the door to any lock. Or, at any rate, is the first step to divorce by mutual consent, and through it even the longest kiss undergoes severance, terminating the lips. Here we go, I'll try. Not to be tied down, Liberty, protect me: Speed my words, and urge your flighty miracle!

"'All right, I love you,' I admitted. We grew healthy again; in record time; startling the doctors. The oxygen box opened up, the hospital door opened up, and we were expelled from both. We walked, a few inches apart, down a public street. We each tilted our heads toward the outside, for a little private independence, including separate breathing. 'Who can tell the kisser from the kissed?' we both were caught saying at the very same time. So here we were being simultaneous again. Fearing that she and I would get mutually married by that method, I made a hurried excuse and slipped away, running as fast as my pants could carry me — in hot pursuit. Although I dodged, it very naturally caught up. 'No!' I said, prepared to attend my death alive. It attached itself to me, and held me tight in its impassioned grip, until the girl came up from behind to join us. The kiss was sort of our pimp, but how amorous! Although already uniting us, it was intent on remaining. It exacted toll tax from us both, so its internal revenue blew up, and we were wet and soaking all over. This dried up our romance, and without stopping to get married, we underwent a lifelong separation, equivalent, in any man's language, to a divorce. During its duration, we abstained from all kissing, internal, external, or even eternal, as the case may be. I had to pay her alimony — kisses — on the installment plan. My lips are rubbed thin, from barrages of lipstick and blood, and the impassioned persistence of an enemy's front teeth. The pressure is off, but her memory whimpers up close. Her scented breath still lingers to mine, and our front skulls merge, the face pressed against a face, brief love's head-on affront. She's amputated off, torn violently; that operation has imposed on me my permanent loss; but the imprint of our tender joining is stamped onto our spirits. Love's portal is at the lips, and the depth of passion is prolonged in a kiss. So pucker up tonight, friends; the lips make the first big impression, and limping lust brings up the supreme rear. With so great a frontal assault, so well supported from behind, we have impotence shipped; attack, my stalwarts! on to the enemy's breach. Admit the lasting impress of a kiss, and boldly we're backed up in big behind. Grind on, men."

Voluminous applause filled the hall. Gala curtain calls implored the speaker to come forward, with the conquering mien of a prince. How proudly he received this ovation!

So grandly exposed, however, he was riddled by some slight criticism. The presence in the story of his "friend," on the telephone, was deemed unnecessary, as not contributing to the action; this superfluous character had operated only as a distraction, and interfered with interest in the kiss, that interminable kiss that had been so binding for the two participants. But at large, the story was vigorously praised, and received glowing tribute. The immensity of the success was undeniable. How many smiles testified to this!

How fabulous that Monday, so glittering its crown! It deserved fame that endured in the annals of the Love Club.

Then a dreary week followed, the invariable letdown. The next scheduled speaker cursed his luck, to succeed so unqualified a success and be a minor sequence in the wake of an eventful landmark. It defied all competition, so he changed the subject entirely, as an evasion of inevitable comparison. He stood up briskly, and made a brisk delivery. It was short, and to the point; in its way, it did admirably, on its own merit. Nor was the applause stinting, at the end. Here it was:

"The body without the girl, I thought, fell short of the ideal. It was hers, her body all right, but she certainly was somewhere else, and was not enjoying it. It seemed strange without her, and wholly unreal. Like a tranquilizer which a corpse imbibes, to escape nervousness. When I finally woke up, after not sleeping all night, only the girl was there, but her body was withdrawn. 'Which one do you like?' she asked. I was too tired to answer."

"A nice fable," said a nondetractor, during the session of general commentary. The slight sermon was bandied about in a round of pros and cons, evoking aimless discussion and generating a scattered chorus of mild debate. It was an "off" Monday, in a sedate, relaxed atmosphere. By no stretch of the term might it be called unpleasant. No explosions, no shouts, but gentlemanly discourse. Gradually the evening waned, and the members voted to go home. Not even a snore of dissent was heard in all the assembly. It was an interval for tiding over, to recuperate from last week's enormous blast; rarely can a blowout be repeated, to shake the foundations of a small week; time must restore the blood pressure, and revive the sleeping sperm. All in nature's rhythm, the tempo of the human mating instinct. Moderation blessed its divided ends, with patched-up intermediary means.

Ah, generous tranquillity, the breath of soft delight!

As usual in the process of subdivided time, another Monday proceeded to arrive. Its existence couldn't be mistaken, nor its veracity be disputed. All civilized men were in agreement on this point, in a world grown speedily uniform. Swiftly the news spread, and the acceptable standard of Monday was confirmed at every hand, and held in prevailing currency. It was authentic, raised eminently above the authority of mere rumor. The consent was universal, so Monday seated itself on its legal throne, to rule as king for a day, in the regal sanctuary of certainty. Its overthrow by Tuesday could only be proclaimed by an act of the future; but time was conservative, as yet.

Careful to establish continuity, the new lecturer was to maintain ties with the last sermon by referring to erotically induced tiredness, and the loneliness that love can carnally furnish, to augment a psychic solitude. A joint isolation connected the partners in the foul deed of love; the lust that bound them broke them apart, sent them spinning into separation. Contact was forbidden to the soul, though thrown like a bone momentarily in grant to the body. This was the depressing theme; all in a setting of physical exhaustion, the narrator's heat-lost saturation which his cunning mate foiled with the wiles of the bed. It was told in a rich poetic style, in a rather stately majesty of English. It commanded a vast dignity, in such formal cadences that greater stature was accorded to the listeners, to make them worthy of so sonorous a sermon. The Love Club's haughty members were now an exalted brotherhood, privileged in exclusive snobbery to be the proud audience to whom were addressed these finely intimate words sprinkled in the splendor of defeated sex:

"When I finish off my woman — it never fails — a relaxed feeling overtakes me. I gently employ this incentive as a ruse with which to woo sleep. When the prelude of the first dream raises its curtain, a hand from the live world, belonging to the mate at my side, pulls the theater down and restores the staleness that had eased my retirement. I turn to her, and ask 'What?' 'Again,' she commands, while my flattened vigor sighs from its deflated pump of emptiness. 'I can't,' I calmly shout. She protests with open cruelty. Mildly violent, I hurt her. So agreeable a sensation promotes her fiendish gratitude, and we converse through love. I throb with more brutality, which she, in her passivity, drinks in. Our unity breaks, in its brittle components of separate division. Her last thought is that she must rest, spanned by our mile's distance. 'Lost!' I complain, and in the solid yard of myself share what room remains with the spaces of loneliness. Let her invade that stony retreat. She'll not, while an inching light gropes deeply into morning's kingdom."

Thus ended the speech, a recital of some of the problems connected with mature love. The Club members drew from their own experience to puzzle out knowingly the universal sum from the speaker's assortment of meaning-driven words, so relevant to the plight and dilemma of each listener. A respectful silence ensued, instead of a volley of questions. Thought moved in the masculine air, between the ceiling and the seated heads. No drink was served, in respect for this somber spell of contemplation, the strenuous leisure of minds at work. Nor was the evening dissipated by another note, until a unanimous motion broke up the session by voting that each and sundry should go home.

Next Monday was now, and a new speaker addresses the group. In love, or its act, is the word-laden mind part of bodily substance, or apart, divided by deed? Is behavior deflated by an inflated mentality of words? Instead of resorting to a first-person method, the deliverer of the speech filled in the shadow of his theme by this ambiguous dialogue, airing the faintness incorporeally phantomed by two indistinct voices:

"'I don't want to end something I can't start,' said the reluctant sexual partner. 'Well then,' said his or her nonmate, 'bring your wares elsewhere.' 'Will you be there?' 'I probably will or won't.' 'Can you make up your mind?' 'It's not my mind, it's my body.' 'Please don't act so fresh.' 'It's not action, it's only talk.' 'Yes, but dangerous talk.' 'Are you always so word conscious?' 'No, but my body is.'"

This was greeted with confusion. What had the dialogue conveyed, if not a mixed intent? Would the author kindly decipher, and unearth the well-concealed message? He defended himself by appealing to humor, and invoking its inexact code, wherein precision was not accurately defined. "It means what you think it means," he confided; and the audience was restless, starved for some respite from doubt.

They grumbled; nor was their dissatisfaction appeased, by any turn or trick. The lecturer became deservedly unpopular, and a bill to oust him from membership in the cult was defeated, despite its justice, by a constitutional clause against unsportsman-like haste in matters of communicable misunderstanding. Thus the motion was desisted from, and good standing in closed ranks, to his great relief, was retained by so ungifted a speaker, who had composed a dialogue so vaguely blurred, so repellent to the good form of easily imagined simplicity, free from that thief of comprehension, ironic subtlety, with its deforming nuances that cripple sense. The villain of this composition was hooted off the rostrum; seeking anonymity among his hostile fellows, he was jostled by the mob, and was a bit roughly handled for not telling a tale straight and spinning a good yarn. How costly was this lesson to his self-esteem! He renounced intellect, and conformed to the current depravity of taste.

The next topic was declared: eyes and women; love's eye-route to its more rooted base, the end sighted by way of the means. The speaker was announced.

"A girl in the full glory of her lipstick gave me a half-surrendering emotional wink, bathing me momentarily in a costly cascade of the most inspired department-store mascara. Reduced to naked eyes, though, she was forced to flee, in shame for her expensively protected modesty, which had been squandered, in a single orgy of dissipation, on worthless me."

By appealing more directly to the senses, and letting the abstractions go hang, this narrator earned a rousing reception, which favorably compared with the ignominy of the previous week's refinement of foolish failure. Outcries of tribute escorted him back to his seat; then there was a hush, and critically the listeners wondered what the theme had been. What, obviously, was the upshot? That cosmetics give women confidence? Nonsense! But why think? Weekends with their hectic schedules of pleasure, transferred sinners, their faculties exhausted, into Monday nighters exposed to varied irregularities of formal verbal trumpetings; and most meanings were hideously complex. Storytelling is a simple art, theoretically; but in practice, the audience is damned.

A new Monday followed, having waited out the week. Officially, the subject, pending development, was love via the sight: How do the eyes reduce the distance between men and women; how does the effect alter the cause, and open the eyes? The listeners sat back, and began to see, while the speaker, squinting hazily, sputtered out:

"One day I caught a cold in my eye, and the doctor recommended winking. I left his office, and strolled down the street. A woman came from the other direction. (She usually does.) I winked, and she took it personally. Catching my infection, she applied the similar remedy, having been a home nurse. We stopped and communicated by wink signals. This entangled our eyelashes, like the horns of two fighting elks. We sought a marriage counselor. Bearing the important honesty of his trade, he demanded to review our license. 'Can't we improvise?' I asked him. 'You mean you're single?' He clipped us apart with one of his legal scissors. The swollen pain gave us the blindness that love requires. 'Are we divorced, or annulled?' the woman promptly inquired. Holding my eyelids steady so as not to wink, I managed one of those difficult smiles which emergency brings into our life. 'I can't see straight,' I informed her, 'but just how pretty are you — are you, for example, ideal?' Modesty blushed from her primrose lips — I detected this from my sense of hearing, since my eyes were undergoing private mental surgery. Her silence was so sexy, I immediately fell in lust. I leaped out of my skin, while unbuttoning every inch of clothing all the way. She couldn't help but notice, and asked for alimony. This crushed my purity, and wounded my thrift. Smiling somewhere between her teeth, she told me that nothing was free."

A wise roar of laughter spread out. Yes, women were that way, all right. Eyes were dangerous instruments, but physical possession had marital implications or blundered into monetary commitments. Women, no sooner seen but desired, set up a social price in return for their dear favors. Pleasure is the most costly commodity.

The Love Club met without reference to season, though members vacationed for summer trips or were otherwise absent due to the severity of winter colds. Meetings were never postponed in case of sparse attendance. Love's business was year-round, without letup. The complications were endless.

The Club was located in the center of town. For all but suburbanite commuters, it was conveniently accessible. Membership conferred prestige, and a conspicuous network of secrecy gave off intimations of a hidden glamor redolent of a magical cult of the exclusive. Dues were collected to keep the organization going. Extensions were planned, lobbyists were hired, and the society held ambitions to expand until its growth commended it as a political bloc. Love would become a power, and its issues would be discussed as national problems, with international repercussions. Was not love every ounce as important as war? Didn't commerce flow through it, and wasn't the economy, in part, based on it? Love flowered to ramifications on a scale eminently universal, and even sent out cosmic offshoots beyond the perimeter of the known. Metaphysically, love had its ultimate roots in God; man, its by-product, was considered its key exponent; and women shared in the considerable glory, as a generous concession by men when sparks of divine weakness strengthened their resolve. Love was on the map to stay, and no life was said to be complete without partaking in its restorative, generative, and purgative effects. Though primitive, love's customs permeated to the intricacies of civilization. Even laws were established, and works of art arduously constructed, to honor its reign and sway over man's immense emotions. Love's place on the map of the world was here permanently to stay, unless dislodged by agents of the diabolical, in which case, hell surely would be unloosed. Such theology was under the jurisdiction of the Love Club. The occult and the practical alike constituted its unflagging duties, its crusade to affix love on an exalted sphere, despite fornication's undenied place on the face of the world's realism. The Love Club dealt with dreams, not only such carnal deliriums as effaced the image of its purity. Wasn't love, all in all, everything? Then to be obsessed by it was only rational, even in such a moderate scheme as entailed the percentage of all. Love was a full phenomenon, as its enthusiastic addicts would flock to testify, on oath of the painful truth. Those who were devoted to love, joined the Love Club; but they must be men.

Last Monday's topic showed how a visual impediment, or infirmity, led nearly to so binding an entanglement that loss of bachelor status, and of money itself, was dangerously close to sight, with its blinding penalties. A new Monday had arrived, bringing forth a fresh speaker, vigorous and virile. He began with the eyes, and worked his way down to the groin level, where love erects its bridge to bind two shores. Here's how he proceeded:

"After eating too many carrots, I began to see too much. Logic afforded the first solution: to close my eyes. But I'm not self-sufficient, so I asked a friend to help. He blindly came to my rescue, but succeeded only in closing his own, which left me completely in the dark. Coming to my sense (and having gotten rid of my friend, that useless nuisance), I began to see visions, concrete dreams with true appearances, reality dressed as image. This was so alarming that for my next meal I avoided carrots altogether, and was struck with vitamin deficiency. I appealed to a doctor, who merely shook his head sadly, and grinned out loud. The nerve!

"But I didn't stay indignant for long, as my body commanded me to lead it, the blood warming to the occasion and, keeping the right muscles in mind, circulating with decorum. To prove my stamina, and abet my flow, I arranged a vital date inside my girl friend, whose clothing she had had the tact to take off. There I struggled against invisible odds, shaking with frenzy. In the end, I suppose, she won."

Chuckles approved this rowdy tale, this bawdy yarn of fun. Rows of teeth shone in the luminous Monday meeting hall, relit once the speech was done. However, there were some adverse comments. The presence of the "friend," in the first paragraph, seemed superfluous to the story: even his uselessness hadn't substantially contributed to the action, which should be keen and swift, an inexorable passage through a narrative retailing of events and culminating in the climactic orgasm with which the brief piece ended. But what has love to do with literary criticism? It should be guaranteed immunity, as a thing apart. Words were but words; sensation could actually be felt, and the flesh was easily sensitive to touch. Had the hero of the tale resorted to carrot-eating again, to give his sight a brilliant luminosity? Or was love but an act of darkness, a blind groping for an essentially evil contact? Was night its daily province, while owls witnessed from the unshaded window? Or isn't sex a sunny act, a pre-star feast? The subject was likely to be continued. Lights dimmed, until Monday was renewed again, allowing for a lapse of a week's interval, along the orderly chart of measured time. How well punctuated in even strokes were these periodical durations! The precision was mathematical, on astronomy's cadenced authority, in beats of yearly eternities. How fatal was the next Monday, and historically appropriate!

Amid fanfare came in the predestined day. The meeting was called to order at the usual time in the evening, a program undeviated from. Striving for continuity, the speaker wore spectacles. He wanted to prove an old adage, to wit, the blindness, proverbially, of love, trite as it may seem. Can love operate without sight, and ply its unseen functions, with mechanical imprecision, in the utmost blackness of the night, which not the slightest star or starriest bulb can, by illuminating, alleviate? The answer was in his story, which he entitled, *Bright Proof of Love's Blindness*. The audience settled back, in postures eager for enlightment. Would they see the point?

"One albino, who had weak eyes, married another albino, who had weak eyes. Even in the dark, unlike owls, they had great trouble seeing. They tried to have conjugal relations of the legal bed. But neither could locate where, in each other. They tried to find their matching parts together, but lacked even instinctual vision. Thus, even physically, love is blind."

Discrimination being ugly, no one laughed: an albino was in

attendance who would wear a pink blush of offense. Not one clap was heard, in deference to the wounded feelings of a minority member, since the Love Club was democratically nondenominational, operating on a policy of liberal antiprejudice, founded on the broad principles of desegregation. Out of delicacy and tact, no mention was made of the story, nor was a single glance directed at the nonplussed white head of youthful embarrassment. Is it a crime to be white? The pulse of one man's shame vibrated among his red-blooded fellows, to spoil the assembly for that evening, In collective guilt, those sturdy brothers went home: in their bedrooms, the light went on, to locate the vital parts of girl friends or wives. Why take a chance, and risk total darkness?

This was their identification with the unfortunate albino. Nor could they trust their eyes. Deep inside, they were assured of final contact, the dreamy touch. There, the feel found a close heaven with bliss for they had been securely met.

Once out, they became puritanical. It came to seem that to abstain was to reduce the stain, and that to strain for restraint, even under pain, was a discipline nobility couldn't afford to disdain. For a brief fashion, a vogue of platonic romanticism sprang up; they would look a girl's character up and down, and fall in virtue with her. Platonic orgies were held, virtuous revels; chivalry came in style again.

Holding hands was considered slightly scandalous, even under Victorian standards. The body was unmentionable; love meant the duty to suffer, an opportunity to mortify the passions it set aflame. Love imposed a rigorous ideal of frustration, and one must be austerely miserable, stoically deprived of the darling illusionary fruits of gratification. Desire would have to be crushed, and agony inserted in its stead. This code of conduct seemed like fun; the members of the Love Club revolted against pleasure's tyranny, and unyoked themselves of bondage to sensual indulgence. They were liberated from being men, to become freely either gods or fools, in their experimental wisdom. Sex was completely taboo, a primitive crime against civilization. It was so foul that even in hell its immorality was legion; only the lowest fiends, lost immortally, could creep in vile appetite to a burning deed that couldn't cool off their ardor; what they committed in the name of love thrust holiness back billions of years, to a pre-evolutionary level; it was evil pollution that they were spreading: would the contagion catch on to the innocent animals, and depopulate the fields of paradise forever? Thank God for God, who'd call a sin black; if religion is the price of redemption, why, it's a cheap bargain, at that. Piety was all the rage to a fanatical extreme beyond the Greek pagan ideal of moderation. And lust was a worse abomination than murder in the range of man's diabolical capacity. Conscience was on the upswing, while guilt was depravity's barometer, a sure giveaway. Love underwent a new definition.

Women were changed, too. They were like dummies, not real or alive. As idols without hair on their flesh, and without flesh on their frame, they were lifted into pure inaccessibility and idealized beyond the remotely pallid circumference of nature. Only a bloodless form was worthy of love, a well-censored transcendence that perfectly obeyed the rigid denials implicit in the severities of puritanical strictness. Indications of a lewd bestiality were held against a woman's virtue; for a woman to seem human was a resounding vice – an incredible offense against even the least requirements of decency: an absolute outrage that no relative spark of leniency would ever condone. So next Monday's speaker fell in love with a dummy, who "lived" (if that's the word) in a department store. What happened in due course of that ill-fated romance, which consumed more than five years of patient pining and melancholy yearning, is the subject of that discourse, or confession, which he delivered in so self-pitying a manner that the audience was basked in tears, drenched in pathetic water streaming from their ducts. The hall was choked with sentimentality while reason fled. Never was woman so glorified on a papier-mâché pedestal; this saga of doomed love had a generous effect on the nobler emotions. How true to life it was, not a painted stage for the histrionic paintings of an ideal: the speaker was revealed as very alive, compared with the object of his fancy, the image most real to the sentiments that fluttered in his heart, like soft-feathered birds restless in a cage of rusty wire and spaces of sacred air:

"I flirted with a window dummy. She was nude but frigid. The night watchman wasn't looking. But I couldn't get in the window. I stood with a moon on me. The night was hot and warm. I put on my favorite wink. She appeared unmoved. But I am not a mannequin, and I felt the cold rejection. A policeman briefly interrupted us. Five years later I returned. Jail had mellowed me. But she wasn't in the window. Whoever had her, I hoped that at least she had clothes on. In her place was an article of empty furniture. Behind me, a lamppost glared down: a false but constant moon.

"The even-tempered sun replaced the hostile scene. The gay sidewalk was spanking with beams. Shadows and their substance walked the human pavement. The bark of a dog, like a cough approved by the doctor, fell on lighthearted ears. Each iron building, square like a lawyer, dry with practical years, kept insisting it was a tree. Our city April, like a burst of natural birth inside a cage, could point to a rare sparrow and to a smile carefully disposed behind someone's teeth. Not even a dirty flower; not even a stubborn rainbow.

"The season slowly improved and grew fat with its fame. Benches were reserved months in advance; and the park seemed a great display of all that weather. The shadow-frowning trees, reflecting office windows, looked sadly mismatched in their zoo, and naked without a nest. Cooing couples, in withered puffery like pigeons, soiled the forbidden grass.

"I balanced a sneeze from my nose and returned it to the distracted pollen. The stores were boasting their sales. Seeking my dummy, I moved like a regretful shopper. Every window echoed another.

"Memories of bars lengthened the waning shadows. Jail had played corruption in me and staggered my sense to be amazed. I calmly found her again. Time, like a solid wedge, forced our hearts apart. In the window, where she wore silks, the early and empty moon made a slow mockery, showing her fashionable enlargement of status against my own frame, reduced from pulse to wire, where nostalgia, decayed like a pigeon, kept its lonely cage. The bloated moon fell upon her face, and the reflection wiped away her character. As a cloud escorted the moon from the scene, my love was only a blur of blankness."

The Love Club was a smudge of sobs, a broken weaving of tears, a weeping moan; its members, in a unison of compassion, cried copiously, melting hardness with liquid groans genuinely heart-felt, not dissembled or counterfeit. What rapport of story with audience: the communication had been total, a mood multiplied without loss from one mind to all. It provoked the comment, "One touch of love makes the whole world mannequin," which was not unaccompanied by some tear-stained smile, though hardly of the jovial kind. It was a moving occasion.

Next Monday was to be a joint performance, a dual effort, instead of the usual solo stint. It would be a lightning dialogue, in which the entertainers would alternate line by line, in witty retort, each completing what the other had added, in turn, and being extended in united progression. Frankly, the subject was sex, with allied pathways of gender in its undiluted admixture. It was really to be an intellectual treat, the likes of which were rare as the earth was presently shaped. All members were sure to attend, with minimal absenteeism, so fine a show had been publi-cized. To miss it would be a disgrace; the Love Club was in full session on a grand occasion. It was becoming increasingly memo-rable, even before the performers had gone through their stunt. Expectation throbbed, like a humming hive of electricity. What magnetism cruised the air, in buzzing glows and other vibrant overtones! A yawn would have been blasphemous, and the culprit bodily ejected from the thronged room. Now was the stage lit, and from either corner of that dramatic curtain emerged one half of this frenzied dialogue. A colorful bril-liancy marked this spectacle for the unforgetting envy of all posterity. The triumph of the twentieth century was announced!

Attention was undivided, in a concentrated ray of focus.

The atmosphere was indeed tense. Grown men were pre-pared to faint in the heat of the suspense.

Now had all relativity vanished in the clean sway of the Abso-lute!

One performer was distinguished from his partner (referred to as B) by being called A. The other, known as B, could be told apart from *his* partner by the latter's nominal name of anonymity. A. Each was different from the other in the same similar way; they shared this difference as whay they most mutually had in common. By common form of precedence, A spoke first, B followed, and so on – but A ended, bringing the cycle back to its original conclusion. A stood at one side, B on the other. They would double in and by opposite polarity multiply one indefinitely. Between them was a link of infinity, a bond for their joint participation. Two would become one, as a limitless factor. Was eternity listening?

A: Why do you chase the girls?
B: Well, aren't they good to squeeze?
A: Has your answer turned girlish with a question?
B: Is flesh understood to be sensually sexy?
A: Yes, passion's modest sheet sheet clothing.
B: A kiss bridges girl – and boy – opposite banks.
A: Love is lust's inhibited dream.
B: Drives are repressed into romance.
A: Orgasms follow, but they don't lead.
B: Ah, how empty is pleasure's core!
A: Arms embrace living ghosts . . .
B: Within sensation's anarchy . . .
A: Death blindly throbs with birth.
B: Pimp us gently together, God.
A: Your children are twinned by their intimacy.
B: Nature owns a growing profit,
A: Converts us to business ends
B: Whose occupation is to meet.
A: Ah, delirium, protect me,
B: The skin's tyranny is hard and deep.
A: Or softly frozen over with warmth.
B: Hold me, the coming's so good,
A: As energies overrun me, and I'm gone,
B: One man, a medium of mankind,
A: Ancestored by the ancestors to be.

Never had an ovation so stirred an excited pulse as was that of the rank-and-file mob which constituted membership in the Love Club. The applause lasted a conservative fifteen minutes, or twenty at a radical guess. What had just been heard was called the finest catechism in the history of ultrareligious profanity, by a pair of eloquent laymen. Outside of proper church Mass, it was the most provocative secular invocation to God that the Almighty had yet ignored from His out-of-hearing height. Mysticism was allied to sex, and they romped together in holy heartiness and a righteous license of an exalted and profane bliss. God benefited mightily from this, and His kingdom was augmented by enriched properties. His capitalistic monopoly was appalling.

A week created another Monday, but the speaker was embittered with age. In grumbling mock despair, he reviewed how his life fluctuated from hate to its alternative, love. The pendulum, even now, swung him from one to the other with its retrospective regularity. Was he bowed with heavy regrets? How did he look back; and when breath takes its final leave, driven from his wind-dry lungs, on what mood will he be perched? In a croaking voice, he stoops back into the dim land of recall. Life is exhumed on the visible intellect of his tongue. On wings of hate and love, his past rises on its low informative flight. What will his gnarled years reveal, remote from hopes of his frail youth? Mentally what will he conclude?

"As I sat waiting to be loved, my life fled by. When I had amassed an age totaling forty, I sat waiting to be loved. When I was seventy-five, I gave up. My earlier failures had been enthusiastic, with plenty of gay despair. Love would always come. I sat, secure and comfortable, waiting for it.

"Hate came at an early age. My clearest memories command it. Rage was close to nobility, and I hated with great dignity. Then the hate went away, exhausted in the fury of its objects. What replaced it I had hoped would be complacency. Now, I'm old. There's no use.

"I remember my early love. Equal to a flower she was. A silly comparison, and as always I lost. A habit, compiled as lifetime.

"Would hate outlast love, in my graveward direction? I have entertained both, and with politeness they have ignored me.

"Perhaps hate achieved my greater aggression, and the passive passion for soft love used up all the patience I had. Now, I can rage."

The audience didn't stir. Is that what their senior member had forecast? The cult of failure and a creed of pessimism had been preached. This sullen message would be rejected by the wholesome taste with aims of aspiration. But does love breed hate? How does frustration heap revenge on a despised cause? One must psychologically deliberate. On what process are emotions transformed, in the wild seasons of their sequence? Can love be stored up? Or does hate wait, like death, to terminate (or pass on, in grim relay) this cycle of roughly flayed edges that flap with vague momentum? In short, where does love lead on its uneven journey along the mind's jagging wilderness? Must even love's essence alter its time-ridden nature? A new Monday would solve the riddle, or increase it. The speaker, a psychiatrist, hacked out an abstract entry into this diseased problem of emotion Can he chart the route of man's earth?

"Love spoils other emotions, like a king greedily eating his mirror. Whoever we love is destroyed, if not slaughtered, by our love's self-devouring excess, until love corruptly flees from its object, and the beloved, left free, becomes herself in a fit of person. Then the love we had, like a passion all fatal, kills the reflection of its own death, and dies mortally affected. One by one, the sunrise of other emotions resumes, especially that ignored one, hate."

"Oh," said the members of the Love Club, suitably enlightened. But what was love? The speaker had omitted its definition, though treating its symptoms with skimpily prescribed remedies. Which are: "Don't bother." His diagnosis was a masterpiece of professional negligence. So his heedings were soundly ignored by the lay public. They'd carry on in the usual way.

Love could be very simple. Advice is out of place. Just mount the girl, and –

But why were there wars? Only an army officer could explain

that and the Club boasted one in its membership file. He was summoned forth and told to pretend to be Mars, the war god who finds time out to probe inside the love goddess, Venus. Then love's relation to other forms of violence, such as hate, murder, and war, might be clarified, and peace reap profit. Why did men kill? Why, too, did they fornicate? Is one's love-mate also one's hate-mate? – they'd tie up, in a stalemate. In his identity of war and love, the officer of arms places his imagination on the crucial territory, that battle of conflict, deploying his forces in an offensive thrust, while contriving on all available fronts, with the material at hand, to speed lovingly the attack, and converge on love's death.

"Being born, Venus discarded her half shell and turned to love. Strange, she picked me. As Mars, I showed her a good time, until her crippled husband wove a brilliant net. What was left? I warred. Now, only the hydrogen can do, anything less fails to be sufficient. You see what love leads to? As a mature adult, my instinct melted into my reason, I've run out of excuses. Blood wants blood, that's all. Ruin all creation. Created, then destroyed. Because whatever is built up can be torn down. Because the new replaces the old. I fail to explain. Yet the deed explains all; hostility, hatred, converts love from what it was to what it's meant to be, wants to be intended for. My logic can be faulted, but I record, and what happens is so. Bad energy in the air endangers future babies, because bombs are no longer only immediate, but eat up the time to come. Is this right? I'm not empowered to answer, but wish Venus would return. With her, a couch and a bed foiled the hour of sleep, and surely the aching moment was golden. I explain what I am: war. But what is war? Ask Jupiter, he's the boss. I go crazy if I think. I only itch to fire, to squeeze the gun. Mankind is enemy. I urge to destroy, and live my happy game a long life. But Venus, she's gone. She would replace war, or abet it. Thinking is not my game, but I get a commission for death. I lack good words, but a world of men reads the clarity of eloquent persuasion into my fiery expression. I'm appealing, I know. Just one Venus, but bring her back. Only return her. I sell all my triumph, and add any bonus, to clash into her arms again. Where all violence melts, and war is softened, a gentle pressure exploding its gun. Meanwhile, I'm a bomb, and am afraid to blow her up. The girl is old now, that proud queen, ruler of wombs for future warriors. War and love. That's my game."

He was in civilian clothes, the officer, but his rank was colonel, or, rumor had it, general. In stiff, rather martial bearing, he left the platform, leading first with a portly belly and trailing behind with his white, well-trained hair. Would Venus, should she return, feel anew the same old love for him? She'd be a hag herself, now.

And where is she, along with all former love? Time's most tragic victim is said to be love. The following Monday would contain a dirge or mourning for the past, a keening wail; the speaker, all alone, would bemoan what he'd lost, tortured by insubstantial memory. Who can but pity his outcast state? All jocular gaiety had abandoned the Love Club; it was a trying period.

Now Monday was here, and a pall of gloom heavily saddened the atmosphere with depressed melancholy. A man so old he was bent, yet not far removed from youth, barely past his teens, came upon the stage. He looked morosely at the audience, and inflicted his sympathy on them. At the proper time, he spoke:

"I've lived almost exclusively in the past, so far, despite my well-diminished future. Whenever anything happened in the past, I generally call it a memory. However, I've already forgotten it. Which adds a nostalgic dimension, and sweetens the mystery. Not that I care. But I'm loyal, you know?

"As I recall youth, generously dipped in pain, a live woman, colored by herself, steps forward, enhancing her slow substance. Into my arms, as it were. But those cold arms, securing her embrace, belong not to me, but, through prolonged amputation, to an almost impersonal past, in which I was my own relative, distantly related to myself as I am today. A blood relative, as it were, from my mother's excellent stock. How I envy him. No wonder my pain is unbearable. Absolutely. Of course. Now, *that* me really had something. He had her. And I, I have it. What?

The memory, well removed, that's what. At most a dim consolation. Frightful yet natural. How inferior we are today. How short is death, and how intimate. A wonder it doesn't shut me off altogether. From some woman, embraced by arms I no longer know, or even claim to own. We are poor now. The poor cousin to the past. Gaining scraps. What a delicate nutrition I have. And how well fed formerly. As I said, I live foreshadowed in an ever rounded memory, in whose pure sunny serenity I quite dismally fade. And not fast enough, either. I should go, at once, poof! Then where will *she* be? In another's memory? I can't take the chance. So I love, and belong to her. As the arms enfold. And I am my former flesh, just now panicking in warmth, on her shattering entrance. Surely it can never live. Once is ever too many, a happening so rare that memory deepens, staggers, and refuses to believe itself. I call it to reality, quite detached from it. There always was a her. Of that I'm sure. Convinced, bridged over the sea of doubt, into the assurance of now. This is a bitter faith. But keeping me alive, it secures for me a lasting function. I operate, and am. And guard my memory, though I am frail and open, sickened by elements. Weaker, as a vessel, than the memory it contains. I'm poorly reduced, like the porter to a former rich man, who used to be himself. What a comedown. No honor. Where's my pride? In those arms, there. Where once such an embrace occurred. Unforgettable. In fact there she is now. The very woman. And I, I'm the embrace. I do it by memory. Without arms. With a vigor, a strength, that knocks now through itself, smashes past the past, and carries her raping into now, ravished by hands that molest, where formerly they were wanted. By force, squeezing the desperate intensity, instead of the old comfort, the invited and accomplished deed."

The Love Club was silent, and sad. Ends are less fun than beginnings, and it hated to leave on that note. A free-for-all talkathon commenced, and conversation issued from every quarter. The time heralded another Monday out, in a short distance. Love, that inexhaustible topic, was discussed. Love was there to endure, handed from man to man, each of whom prized his own tool. The absent women were everywhere.